A DEATH IN THE LOCH

A EUPHEMIA MARTINS MYSTERY

Caroline Dunford

A DEATH IN THE LOCH

A Euphemia Martins Mystery

Published by Accent Press Ltd – 2014

ISBN 9781783755271

Copyright © Caroline Dunford 2014

The right of Caroline Dunford to be identified as the author of this work has been asserted by her in accordance with the Copyright, Designs and Patents Act 1988.

Chapter One:

Stapleford Hall, where so many memorable and unwelcome adventures have begun.

'I shall be happy to welcome Euphemia back as my housekeeper,' said Sir Richard Stapleford, Lord of Stapleford Hall and my arch-enemy.

'Euphemia is my companion now,' hissed his twin sister Richenda, 'she requires a room *above* stairs!'

Brother and sister faced off across the grand black-and-white tiled hall of their modern 'ancestral' home, built in 1898 with all the vulgarity that their successful merchant banker father could muster. It was now late 1911, and time had neither improved the house nor the tastes of the remaining family members who occupied it. The rug, a fashionable and nightmarish organic design composed of spirals and circles of violently opposing hues that was deplored by all but the upstairs inhabitants, lay between them like some whirling vortex of horror made colour.

'It's all kicking off, isn't it?' said Merry softly in my ear.

'I don't understand,' I whispered. 'Last time I saw Sir Richard he banished me from the house and threatened to excommunicate any member of the family who had any form of intercourse, social or professional, with me. Now he wants me back on the staff?'

'You heard how he bought the Peterfield Property and

got himself a right-hand man, Gilbert Barker.'

I shivered involuntarily.

'I see you've met him,' said Merry. 'If I had a penny for every time he's tried it on with me I'd be richer than the Staplefords.'

'He makes inappropriate advances to you?' I asked, appalled.

'To every girl below stairs. Fortunately my way of deterring him seems to be having an effect. It involves a cooking pot,' she said, tapping the side of her nose. Seeing my horrified face, she added, 'I only hit him in the head. Nowhere it's going to do any damage.'

'Merry, you can't! You'll be dismissed and charged with assault!'

'I've got all the girls keeping a pot handy.'

'Aren't you afraid that one of them might accidentally hurt him quite seriously?'

'Nah, he's a tall chap and the girls are all much shorter. It's a kind of up-swing action.' She demonstrated what looked like a rather wonky tennis serve.

'Merry!'

Merry deflated before me like a puppet whose strings had been cut. 'Oh, all right. I've never actually hit him. I just sort of brandish it like I might. He's fairly confident I wouldn't whack him, but not completely sure. Makes him back down. As for the other girls, they're all far too timid.' Merry snorted. 'Mind you, he doesn't know that. The mere sight of a pot has him backing off like lamb that's smelled mint sauce.'

'I can't think of anyone less like a lamb,' I said. Merry sniggered.

Bertram Stapleford, the twins' younger step-brother, touched me lightly on the arm. 'Perhaps it would be better if we withdrew until my siblings have this matter sorted.'

I smiled at him. It was typical of Bertram to want to take me away from any trouble or conflict even when it was highly impractical. We had arrived but half an hour since from the estate of Richenda's fiancé, the very charming Hans Muller. Our trunks littered the hallway.

'I rather think,' I said, 'that it would be helpful to know whether I am to lodge above or below stairs so I know where to withdraw to.'

'Euphemia,' exploded Bertram, 'you cannot possibly agree to becoming that man's housekeeper again!'

'No,' I agreed. 'If Richenda fails then I fear I must travel on to the local inn.'

'Over my dead body!' stormed Bertram.

'Excuse me, sir,' said Merry. 'I might be able to clear something up here.'

Bertram looked down at her in surprise, but not in anger. Merry had been with the family a very long time, as a maid and since my departure as a sort of head maid and housekeeper combined. Even Richenda liked Merry, whose real name was Mary but was generally so happy she had been christened Merry by the staff and family shortly after she came to work at Stapleford Hall. Bertram was fond of her in a purely gentlemanly way. 'Explain, Merry,' he said.

'I'm not doing bad,' said Merry blushing slightly and casting her gaze down, 'but I ain't Euphemia and I'm certainly not trained to be a housekeeper when we've got guests in. Mrs Deighton's been keeping me right with the food and stuff and the girls have been good at banding together, but Lord knows I can't run the house when it's in full steam. It's been just the staff for ages. Lord Stapleford and Mr Barker ain't been back long and that's been strain enough.'

'Isn't Rory here?' asked Bertram.

Merry shook her head. 'He's still butlering for the Earl until the Earl's own man recovers. Lord Stapleford's racking up a favour. If he had any sense he wouldn't come back here.'

I shook my head. 'The Earl wouldn't poach him like that. He'd wait until Rory was back on staff here before he made him an offer. He'd think it ungentlemanly otherwise,' I said.

'Yes,' said Bertram.

Merry looked over, studying me. She had stood my friend since I first turned up soaking wet seeking a post as a maid, unskilled and untrained. From the sidelines she had watched my meteoric rise from maid to housekeeper to companion. She had stuck with me through the several murders and bizarre deaths that I had so unfortunately encountered, and never once had she shown any jealousy of my position, but she saw something about me was different with a clarity the others lacked. I had never told her the truth, that I was the estranged granddaughter of an Earl and that my meagre earnings were all that kept my mother and little brother from destitution. I was better-born than any of the Staplefords, and more than once Merry had seen that my knowledge of the polite world upstairs was far more extensive than any servant's should have been.

'I'm sure with a little help you would be an excellent housekeeper,' I told her, and I meant it. Merry was bright, if sometimes passionately impulsive.

'Maybe,' said Merry, 'but you're here, and Richard reckons he can have you for free while Richenda stays.'

'Cheap bas –' Bertram broke off with a cough.

'He's having a party to see in 1912,' said Merry. 'It's going to take a lot of work.'

While the three of us had been whispering Richard and

4

Richenda had descended to screaming at each other. They resembled nothing more than a pair of cats squaring up over disputed territory.

'I've had enough of this,' said Bertram, and taking me by the wrist he led me up the stairs past Richard. 'I'm putting Euphemia in the blue bedroom,' he told Merry loudly. He didn't exactly drag me up the stairs, but his hold made it quite clear he was prepared for a scuffle if I resisted. By this time the combination of the shouting and the lurid rug were edging me towards a tremendous headache. I went with him. 'I'll get a footman, if Richard still has any, to bring up your luggage and send Merry with a cup of tea. Then she can unpack for you,' said Bertram, leaving me at the door.

'But Richard ...'

'I doubt they have even noticed we have left,' said Bertram. 'Besides, at some point Richard is going to remember that Richenda has significant shares in the bank now she is of age, and so he needs her onside if he is to continue to control the bank.' He paused. 'If he doesn't, Barker will be bound to remind him.'

Bertram then very properly left me. The blue bedroom, which was one of the nicer guest rooms, did have comfortable seating set around the fireplace, but as a companion and therefore almost a lady, and unrelated at that, Bertram could not stay and take tea with me in my boudoir without arousing comment. It was all so ridiculous. I had worked as his housekeeper at his wretchedly badly built estate, White Orchards, and often been alone with him. More to the point, he had on numerous occasions asked me to marry him, but rather out of a chivalric sense of protecting me from his step-brother's malign intentions than because he loved me. I had, of course, had to say no. I had been engaged for a short time to the absent butler, Rory McLeod, twice, once unofficially and once officially. He was the son of a grocer, utterly unsuitable to someone of my true social status – and the nicest and most handsome man I had ever met.

Despite a rather uncomfortable tendency to jealousy, which I had been sure I would have been able to curb over time, Rory had decided he loved me too much to marry me. Really, sometimes I felt like a heroine in an old-fashioned gothic novel. When I was feeling low I suspected that my story might also have a dark and gothic ending. I was staring out of the window and thinking about the time Richenda had shut me in a wardrobe, just after her father's murder and before we had reached a better understanding[1] when I heard a sharp rap on the door. Without waiting for my response the door flew open and Merry stood in the doorway, clutching a laden tea tray and with an expression of awe on her face. 'Bleedin' 'ell!' she articulated breathlessly, 'they're saying you've only gorn and found another dead body.'

I nodded, 'Two,' I said tonelessly.

'Bleedin' 'ell,' repeated Merry.

'It wasn't my fault,' I said defensively.

'Never bloody is, is it?' said Merry coming into the room and closing the door with her heel. She set the tea tray down on a small table and put her hands on her hips. 'Look, I'm right glad to see you and all that, but will you please not find any more murder victims while you're here. It's becoming an unfortunate habit with you.'

Rightly interpreting that Merry's nose was out of joint because the new lady's maid that had accompanied us

---

[1]Please see my earlier journals for full, and at times lurid, details.

6

knew the full story and was doubtless already holding the kitchen spellbound with the tale, I invited Merry to sit down and join me for tea. I then unfolded the whole tale of my stay at the Muller estate.

'So that's it, straight from the horse's mouth,' I concluded.

'Dunno about that. Richenda looks more like a horse than you do,' said Merry.

'You know what I mean,' I said, biting my lip. Richenda did indeed bear an unfortunate resemblance to her favourite horse. When fighting with her brother her nostrils had positively flared and I would not have been surprised if she had pawed the ground. 'Richenda is improving vastly away from her brother,' I said.

'If 'alf of what you say is true,' said Merry, 'not that I mean you'd be lying, it's just a bit hard to swallow, but there were times in your story when she almost sounded human.'

'I find allowing her access to plenty of cake helps,' I said.

Merry nodded wisely. 'Richenda always improves with cake,' we both said at the same time and fell about laughing.

'And this bloke is really going to marry her?' asked Merry.

'Quite soon, I think. Under the circumstances it will be a small and quiet wedding.'

'Good,' said Merry, ''Cos when she was engaged before and you went to her wedding, people started dying again. And when I say dying I mean murdered.'

I shuddered, remembering the whole ghastly time. 'Look, this time I'm only back for a short time and nothing untoward can possibly happen.'

Merry regarded me dubiously with her head on one

side. 'If you say so,' she said in a disbelieving voice. I threw a pillow at her. As usual Merry dodged.

'As enjoyable as it has been to catch up with your exploits,' she said, 'I for one have work to do. So if madam will tell me which of her trunks she wishes unpacked first?'

'Leave it,' I said. 'It is so deathly dull being a companion I may be forced to take up embroidery. Richenda isn't one for scintillating conversation. I'll unpack them myself. It'll give me something to do.'

Merry looked at me as if I was mad. Clearly she thought she'd love someone to fetch and carry for her. She had no idea what it was like being a single lady. In-between the violent eruptions in my domestic life as a companion I was close to being bored witless. Indeed my happiest times had been working below stairs at Stapleford Hall when I had the running of the house to occupy my time. I sighed. Maybe it wouldn't have been so bad if Richenda had agreed that I would act as housekeeper for the little time we were here. I decided to put this idea to her later.

'No. No! No, you ungrateful wretch,' spat Richenda. 'You are my companion. It would lower my status if you went back to being a housekeeper.' We were the first down for dinner and were drinking cocktails that a footman I didn't recognise had rather expertly made for us.

'This is very pleasant,' I said, quickly changing the subject.

'Hmm,' said Richenda, 'it doesn't taste as if it has any alcohol in it.' Richenda was wearing a tiny band-style hat with enormous green feathers. One dipped into her drink as she sniffed it. 'Damn,' she said brushing it aside and sending droplets down the front of her ivory and green evening dress. 'Damn silly shape for a glass.'

'Damn silly drink if you ask me,' said Bertram, coming into the room and collecting his glass from the footman. 'Almost as silly as your hat, Rich!'

'I'll have you know I had this imported from France!'

'I'm sure they were glad to get rid of it,' said Bertram.

'You are a cad,' said Richenda without rancour. 'What do you know about women's fashion?'

'I heard Mrs Deighton has made her French cream cake for dessert in honour of your arrival, Richenda,' I said.

Richenda's eyes lit up. 'Yum!'

'Don't you want to look …' began Bertram, who encountering a look from Richenda stumbled a little, 'I mean, your wedding and all that.'

'Hans loves me just as I am!'

'You mean he loves your shares,' said a voice from behind us.

'Almost as much as you do,' countered Richenda with unusual wit. 'I'm sure you're eager to remind me of how important family is during my little visit.' She raised her glass to her twin. 'And let me remind you I have made a will, so if I die before I am wed you won't see a penny of those shares.'

Instead of protesting Richard grunted and nodded. 'Clever girl,' he said.

Really, living with these people, was it any surprise one tripped over the occasional dead body?

Chapter Two:

The establishment of status

Richard won the argument by pretending it had never happened. I can't say that mealtimes were particularly enjoyable, but in general the master of the house ignored me. Doubtless biting his lip and thinking of Richenda's shares. Bertram, much in the manner of a man, bailed. Most days regardless of the weather he took a gun out and walked the grounds. One morning he received a telephonic communication. I knew at once it had been his man down at White Orchards.

'Don't say anything, Euphemia,' he warned me as he stalked across the hall where I was trying ineptly to arrange some winter roses. 'Don't say a word.'

I disobeyed at once. 'I didn't say anything,' I said, inaccurately.

'You looked it,' growled Bertram.

I raised my eyebrows.

'Oh, very well, if you insist, my new agent tells me that the inner gable leaves of White Orchards are not substantial enough and will need to be rebuilt.'

'Why do inner gable leaves matter?' I asked, thinking helplessly of terracotta trees.

'They are what the outside chimneys are tied to,' said Bertram.

'With string?'

'God, it's not that bad,' said Bertram. He paused and pinched his nose between his thumb and forefinger. 'Actually, it is. They use metal ties to anchor the chimney and outer gables. It seems the builders who did some running repairs to the house for the previous occupants used soft stone and now it's coming away in handfuls.'

He looked so crestfallen that I relented. 'There was no way you could possibly have known that,' I said.

'No,' agreed Bertram. 'I know. But it means as well as having to attend Richard's awful New Year party, which I had already promised to do, we will all have to spend Christmas here again. I had hoped you, me, and Rich could have escaped.'

'I had hoped Richenda would allow me some time off for Christmas.'

'No hope of that I'm afraid. If she has to stay at Rotten Richard's then she'll ensure we suffer with her. I don't suppose we could all descend on your mother, could we?' asked Bertram.

'No,' I almost shouted. I took a deep breath. 'No, I'm afraid it would be beyond my mother's dwelling as well as her budget to cater for us all.'

'Damn it, Euphemia! I'd rather sleep in a cowshed than suffer one of Richard's parties.'

'It might be exciting,' I teased. 'We could all play wink murder.'

'Don't. Just don't,' said Bertram and slouched off to retrieve his gun.

Concentrating on New Year it turned out Richard had decided on only a small Christmas party for family and close friends. And thus began the row again between Richenda and Richard over my attendance. In the end I took Richenda to one side and reassured her.

'I honestly don't want to be the ghost at the feast,' I

said. Richenda bristled with misunderstanding. 'Your brother is quite right that some of the guests will recall me as a housekeeper and maybe even a few as a maid. I no more want to sit through their questioning or disapproving looks than Richard wants me at the dining table. Of course, I'd be happiest at home ...'

'Impossible,' snapped Richenda.

'But if that is how you feel, allow me to have my Christmas celebrations alone. I have near on a suite of rooms and Mrs Deighton will ensure I am well catered for.'

Richenda sighed. 'Oh, if you must. Just for Christmas Day though, and I shall buy you an extra-large present to make up for it.'

I smiled and thanked her. All the while praying that my present would not be one of her infamous sartorial choices. In truth I had a plan to into invite Merry, Merrit, and a few of the other staff I knew well to my room for a Christmas drink and snatched snack between their duties, but in this I was to be foiled by the sudden arrival of Mrs Lewis.

Richard informed us proudly over breakfast one day that a new housekeeper would be joining his staff. He made it clear she was a paragon of virtue and her references were outstanding. Bertram and I exchanged looks. Neither of us could fathom why such a perfect servant would choose to work in the middle of nowhere for Richard's notoriously low wages.

The answer came when the footman opened the front door later that night and screamed. Mrs Lewis had what could be described, if one was being very generous, as a face with character. As Merry told me later when she came by to turn down my bed for the night, 'Lord, if you met her on a dark night with only a candle for light you'd think the devil himself had come for you.'

'Drinks, does she?' I said thinking of the late and not particularly lamented Mrs Wilson.

'No,' said Merry. 'Well-spoken. Took the time to talk to all of us. She even asked me if I was unhappy about her taking over as housekeeper.'

'What did you say?'

'I said I was bloody well delighted and that I'd only been an under housekeeper under sufferance.'

I laughed.

'And you know what she said?'

I shook my head. 'She said, and I quote (here Merry put on what she thought of as an upper-class accent but which sounded like someone with enlarged adenoids) "In a Christian household, Mary, and I believe this one to be such or I would not have taken the position, one does not swear. However, I am appreciative of both of your sense of duty to your employers that you have been doing your best under difficult circumstances and that you bear no resentment of my arrival. I shall endeavour to return your graciousness by training you up so that one day you will make someone an excellent housekeeper." '

'That's very nice of her,' I said.

'I think she is nice,' said Merry. 'Very formal and very against women servants marrying, though. I've already told Merrit to keep everything on the quiet side. She's formal, but she's fair. I think I can learn a lot from her.'

'Excellent,' I said, already almost half-asleep. 'I must meet her tomorrow.'

'Oh no,' said Merry, 'I really wouldn't do that if I were you.' But I was already half-asleep and thought I must have misheard her.

The next morning it turned out I had heard her exactly right.

It had become my custom to rise earlier than the family

and come down to the kitchen for a cup of tea and a slice of toast as Mrs Deighton cooked up the family breakfast. It gave me a chance to catch up with my old friends and also to hear what was going on in the house. A good servant notices everything.

But this morning when I sat down at the kitchen table as usual Mrs Deighton gave me a startled look. She opened her mouth to say something but the voice came from directly behind me.

'Miss St John! Whatever can we do for you?'

The voice was as commanding as a governess and I leapt to my feet. Turning I saw a tall, middle-aged woman with neat grey hair and a slender figure dressed in black. She was unremarkable except her face reminded me of nothing as much as the gargoyles on my late father's church. My jaw dropped.

'I'm s-s-sorry,' I stammered, 'I didn't hear you approach.'

Mrs Lewis gave me a half-smile that said she appreciated my tact at not mentioning her appearance, but that she saw straight through me. 'Perhaps you would do me the kindness of sparing me a few minutes.'

I looked at her blankly. 'In my parlour,' she said.

'I haven't quite finished my toast,' I said.

'Breakfast for the family will be served in half an hour.'

So that was it. I was to be upbraided for deigning to eat in the kitchen. As soon as we entered her parlour, which had once been mine, I began to explain, 'My situation is a little unusual ...'

'I know,' forestalled Mrs Lewis. 'You have had quite a meteoric career.' This was said completely without resentment. 'But difficult as it is to move up in the world, Miss St John, it is even more difficult to move back down.

I understand that you doubtless have affection for the staff and even number some of them as old friends, but I am afraid that is not a situation I can allow to continue. Mrs Deighton, as I am sure you were completely unaware, is suffering badly from her rheumatism this morning. It is quite a struggle for her to concoct the large breakfast that has been ordered, but she is determined to pull her own weight – which I find admirable.'

'Indeed,' I said quietly.

'If you had still been a maid she would have ushered you out of the way, but as a companion she has no authority to ask you to leave her in peace to work.'

'I would have completely understood!' I exclaimed.

'And she would also have feared that you would think she was spurning your friendship now you work above stairs. As you know, she is a most kind-hearted woman.'

'You're saying I am a liability below stairs,' I said.

'I am afraid so, Miss St John. And I am very sorry to say so, because I imagine your position though now socially superior may be a little lonely, but I cannot have the workings of the house disrupted. It is my duty and my livelihood to ensure a smooth-running house.'

'Of course,' I said horrified to find myself blinking back tears.

Mrs Lewis nodded. 'I knew you were a sensible woman who would respond to plain speaking.' I judged this to be one of her highest compliments and attempted to smile. 'Now,' she continued, 'until our butler returns I must continue to train Archie to practice carrying the third-best crockery and even attempt to convince him to master the art of turkey carving.'

'It will doubtless be so poorly carved the first few times you will be unable to serve it upstairs.'

The gargoyle face broke into a wide smile. 'Indeed, and

he will have to eat the proceeds. Excellent point. Though, to be honest, I do hope and pray Mr McLeod will be returned to us before Christmas arrives.'

In my turn I wondered if Rory McLeod would be allowed to talk to me upon his return and more to the point whether he would want to.

Chapter Three:

Christmas

Much against my wishes, and despite my resorting to begging, Richenda went Christmas shopping in London without me. While she was away Richard and I studiously ignored each other. Merry, to whom I had explained Mrs Lewis's decree, pooh-poohed it with her usual disregard for authority. She continued to visit me for the occasional gossip, but I couldn't help notice that these visits were becoming less frequent. The weather took a turn for the worse to the extent that even Bertram would not go out to shoot. He decided to teach me cribbage, which of course my father had already taught me. I beat him soundly each time and he became quite grumpy. I suggested chess and he agreed. I was still a better player, but as I suspected his rash and unpredictable style of gaming made him difficult to anticipate and therefore difficult to beat. At times his moves were erratic, but on occasion they were brilliant. I appreciated perhaps more than ever before that Bertram had a first-class brain and very little in his life that allowed him to put it to use.

I also discovered that Richard's father must have handed over the stocking of the library to someone else, so that quite by chance there were some excellent books included. What with these, the daily duels of chess, and reading the morning paper, I felt in better mental fettle than I had for years. I even indulged in brushing up a little on my Greek. Bertram did catch me reading it, but fortunately he didn't understand. I suspected Bertram was not strong on languages, ancient or modern. He could be incorrigibly lazy when his interest was not aroused. Both required considerable application and I saw more clearly than ever before this was not in his make-up. I despaired that he would ever find true happiness unless he could find some purpose other than the rebuilding of White Orchards. However, much as I regarded him with affection and even dared to think of him as a friend, there was no way I could ever broach the subject with him. If only he had had the guiding hand of a father as excellent as mine.

Richenda returned two days before Christmas bearing a great many parcels and packages. Around her neck hung a substantial, but tasteful, ruby and gold necklace. 'A present from Hans,' she said blushing. 'We managed to meet up for lunch in town.'

'It is very lovely,' I said honestly, wondering how far her very charming fiancé had managed to charm her and whether I should have insisted more strongly on chaperoning her.

'And terribly expensive,' hissed Richenda, giving a little girlish giggle. 'It's my pre-wedding present. He's still going to buy me a wedding present too!'

'How lovely,' I said repetitively. 'What will you be buying him?'

'Good heavens,' said Richenda, 'I hadn't thought. What does one buy a groom?'

'It depends on the groom. What did you …' I broke off in confusion.

'Buy poor Tippy?' said Richenda, quite unmoved. 'Several cases of wine for his cellar. Tippy was easy. I know I shouldn't speak ill of the dead, and you probably never noticed, but poor Tippy wasn't that bright. His tastes were very predictable.'

'Perhaps an engraved full-hunter pocket watch commemorating the date?' I said, fishing for news of the ceremony.

'Now that is an excellent idea. I shall send you to choose one. Your taste is much closer to Hans's than mine. Much as I love Hans, he is unimaginative.'

Hans Muller had exquisite taste, which Richenda sadly saw as dull. 'I can't buy his wedding present for you!' I said, aghast. 'That's far too intimate!'

'We won't tell him, silly,' said Richenda, twirling her necklace so it glinted, 'and wouldn't you prefer Hans got something he liked rather than something I picked?'

She had me there, but I could hardly say so. Richenda took my silence as acceptance. 'Now come and see what I've got you for Christmas. I know it's two days off, but I can't wait to show you and you won't be joining us for lunch anyway.'

She dumped four hat boxes on my bed and looked at me expectantly. With a sinking heart I unboxed four hats in quick succession, all of them purple and green: a huge straw summer hat, a winter cloche, a band complete with foot-long feathers, and something daring and floppy that Richenda explained was French. 'They all match,' she said happily. 'These can become your signature colours. You will be so stylish.'

Personally I thought I would look like nothing more than a mouldy cabbage, but I managed to swallow my bile and thank her profusely. I also gave her my gift, which was a pair of enamelled earrings, coloured in blues and greens. Although not expensive they were unusual and bright. To my surprise Richenda loved them and even embraced me.

On Christmas Eve Bertram and Richard got drunk. Richenda and I, Richenda also slightly tipsy, helped the staff decorate the big tree in the hall. The tenants had already had their party, but tonight the servants were given their gifts and instead of the Stapleford tradition of giving them new uniforms Richenda and Bertram had persuaded Richard to give them all a small cash bonus. Small to Richard, but very gratefully received.

It was very late, when Richenda and I were on the point of retiring, that the front doorbell rang and Gilbert Barker arrived. Richard and Bertram swept him off to investigate the contents of further decanters, all enmity forgotten with the aid of Christmas spirits.

Richenda and I went to bed.

The next day did not begin well. I heard Richard shouting and grousing. Mrs Lewis delivered my breakfast personally and by her manner rather than her words let it be known she thought it disgraceful I was not to join the family for the festivities. Instead, she promised me a fine meal again delivered to my boudoir. 'Although I am afraid I may not have the time to deliver it myself, and may have to send Mary, who I believe you know as Merry.' She looked at me down her crooked nose and nodded once. It seemed Merry was to be given liberty to keep me company for a while due to the family's poor behaviour. I nodded back. None of this was said between us. I judged Mrs Lewis to be a very shrewd woman and a very fair one too. I wondered how long she would stay in the Staplefords' employ, and indeed why she had ever taken the post in the first place.

'I've been called Merry since I arrived here!' cried my friend as she erupted through my doorway. I dropped my book.

'Merry Christmas!' I said.

Merry gave me a scathing look as she dumped her tray down on my table. 'Are you trying to be funny?'

'No! Er – would Happy Christmas be better?'

Merry threw herself down on the edge of my bed. Tears welled in her eyes. 'It's being an awful Christmas,' she said. 'Merrit's been sent down to Peterfield. I don't know why, but I bet that Lewis hag had something to do with it. She doesn't approve of relationships between staff.'

'Most houses don't,' I said calmly, 'but Richard and Richenda have both made it clear that they have no problem with the two of you being engaged. I think their word counts for more in this house than that of Mrs Lewis.'

'Pah! And she won't let anyone call me Merry. She says I have a Christian name and it's my Christian duty to use it.'

'That does seem a bit silly,' I admitted. 'But from the two plates on the tray I assume she is allowing you to eat with me today. That was kind.'

'Pah,' said Merry again.

'And a small decanter of wine. Shall I pour?'

Merry rummaged in her apron and thrust a small packet out at me. 'It's not much,' she said roughly.

'A present,' I said in delight. Unwrapping it I revealed a small, hand-worked needle case with room for a few threads. It was exquisite, and I said so.

'I know you probably get better things from shops, but I thought being a lady you might have the occasional problem with your gown when you were out, or Richenda might, seeing how clod-hopping she always is.'

'I love it,' I said sincerely, 'and it means all the more to me that you made it for me. I'm afraid I bought your gift.' I handed her a small packet. Merry's face lit up when she found it contained a large number of colourful ribbons. I knew she couldn't afford many personal clothes and often liked to use ribbons to brighten up or change her small wardrobe.

Impulsively Merry sprang up and hugged me, almost impaling us both on my new needle case. Harmony once more restored we sat down to share our Christmas meal. As it remained primarily *my* Christmas meal we had portions from the family table. Mrs Deighton had excelled herself. Merry, who was quite unused to good wine, was distinctly tipsy by the end. In all too short a time she staggered off downstairs, the dishes on the tray sliding ominously from side to side. I chose not to show her Richenda's gift to me as I was quite certain that she wouldn't be able to carry the tray for laughing.

Bertram dropped by and gave me a small mother-of-pearl brooch, shaped like a cat curled into a small contented ball. I thanked him and gave him the gentleman's travel clothes brush I had bought him. He laughed and said, 'This is for when I come in from shooting covered in mud, isn't it?'

'You have been leaving quite a trail after you,' I said, smiling, 'and what should I make of you giving me a cat?'

'I thought it would remind you of home,' he paused, 'you know, all vicarages have cats, don't they?'

We had kept a mouser for the outhouse, but my mother loathed cats and none had ever been allowed inside the house. I suspected a cat was the only creature on God's Earth that could outstare her and she knew it. Aloud I said, 'Of course, how thoughtful of you.' Bertram beamed. Like Richenda he always responded well to praise, no matter who it came from. Their childhoods had been far from idyllic.

And so another Christmas Day passed. I thought of my mother and little brother and wrote them a very long letter.

Merry returned later with a light supper, but this time she couldn't stay. 'Lord Stapleford is like a cat on hot bricks,' she explained. 'That Gilbert Barker's brought important news from Peterfield.'

'What news?'

'As if I care,' said Merry. 'Merrit's back and I'm going to wish him a very *Merry* Christmas!'

Chapter Four:

Should auld acquaintance be forgot (and sadly they rarely can be, no matter how hard one tries)

The time between Christmas and New Year passed very slowly for me. But for everyone else it flew. Richard's New Year party had the staff scurrying in all directions. Every single bedchamber in the house was to be opened up. Merry told me that further guests were to stay at a local tavern only a short drive away. 'This house won't ever have seen so many people,' she said one morning when she came to collect my tea tray. 'I do hope the ballroom floor is up to it. Far as I know it ain't ever been tested. And Mrs Deighton doesn't know if she's in heaven or hell. She's got the finest produce for once. No expense spared. But a mountain of work to do. She's even got to paint gold leaf onto some of the desserts.'

'No,' I said, 'you can't eat gold, can you?'

'Certainly looks like gold. Fine as tissue paper it is. Has to be laid on the cakes ever so gentle.'

'What a waste,' I said.

'Do you think it – er – comes out the other end?'

'Ugh, Merry, not before breakfast! And I have no idea. Why is Stapleford doing all this?'

She shrugged. 'He's mad, isn't he?' She gave me a sly grin. 'Talking of mad, has Richenda bought you a ballgown yet?'

I pulled a face at her. 'Richard has banned me from attending his party, so she hasn't had to – thank goodness.'

'He really doesn't like you, does he?'

'The feeling,' I said, 'is mutual. I can't leave this house soon enough.' Later, I was to regret this rash utterance.

Merry looked a bit hurt. 'I liked having you back.'

'And I like seeing you. Couldn't you and Merrit come and work for the Mullers after Richenda is married?'

Merry shrugged. 'I'll believe in this marriage only after I see the wedding bands on both their fingers. You know the newspapers have christened her "the doomed bride"?'

'None of the papers I read have mentioned that.'

'Well, if this wedding doesn't come off even your posh papers will be calling her that,' said Merry snidely and stomped off.

I suppose I should have been offended that Richard remained determined to deny my existence in his house, but, honestly, I didn't care. Bertram and I managed to spend time together and I saw less of Richenda than I had at the Muller estate, which came as a relief. So much so I had begun to wonder if I was up to being her full-time companion. I needed a position, but being with Richenda fourteen or more hours a day, even when she was in a good mood, could be mind-numbing. I knew she had been interested in the suffragettes, the cause of fallen women, and even the fashionable pursuit of spirituality, but she seemed to have abandoned all this. She could even be witty, but of late she had become determined to be a good housewife and a fashionable lady. It is not fashionable for women, even ladies, to be intelligent – as my mother would tell you. Her favourite phrase was that *intelligence in a girl was about as useful as a pair of hooves*. It seemed to me that Richenda was attempting to follow her example and suppress her intelligence. It was all 'Hans will look after this' or 'Hans will tell me what to do about that'. I had every respect for Mr Hans Muller, but Richenda's decision to become a good little wife was making her exceedingly dull and tiresome. But then, with all the murders and scandal that had surrounded her and her family, who was I to begrudge her a little normality?

Oh, Lord. I must own it. I was bored. Goodness knows I did not wish for a sudden death, but a minor alarm or demanding puzzle would have been very welcome. And again I will reiterate the statement: 'be careful what you wish for'.

New Year's Eve arrived. I was prepared with a good book and a well-banked fire in my boudoir. I had managed to persuade Richenda not to wear the canary yellow headband with her blue and crimson chequered gown. The gown on its own was shocking enough and I was very glad that Hans was unable to make the party. There is only so much an engaged man can suffer before he leaves permanently for the continent. With the removal of the headband her outfit suggested unusual taste, but it would no longer offend the other guests' digestion. I had also on Bertram's advice bolted my door. All in all I felt safe and secure. I had been delivered an early supper so I had no need to see any other person until the New Year dawned tomorrow.

I had reached an exciting part of my novel: the heroine hung by one hand from a cliff edge with no hope of rescue when there came a knock on my door. A glance at the clock told me it was 10 p.m. Dinner would long be over and the guests would be making inroads on the liquid refreshments. Accordingly I ignored the knock. Whoever it was persisted. The knocks became louder.

'I fear you have the wrong room, sir,' I said. I doubted a lady would be so driven by curiosity to get into a locked bedchamber.

'Open up, Euphemia.'

The door muffled the voice.

'Go away,' I said tersely.

'Come on, Miss Martins,' said the voice loudly.

I flew across the room and unbolted the door. No one in this house should know my real name.

Lord Milford, sometimes known as Fitzroy, lounged in the doorway.

'You,' I said as coldly as I could. Milford/Fitzroy was a gentleman in the pay of His Majesty's Government and prone to dealing with delicate political situations. He both knew my real name and my grandfather, the Earl. He should also as a professional have known better than to shout my real name in public. I said as much.

Fitzroy grinned. 'I'm not drunk, Euphemia. I needed to get your attention.'

'You have it for a very short space of time.'

'Don't be like that, Euphemia. Go and put your party dress on. I'm bringing you downstairs.'

'Lord Stapleford has not invited me.'

'Lord Stapleford can go stuff himself,' said Fitzroy amiably. 'You'll be with me.'

'Why on earth would I want to do that,' I enquired tartly.

'Because I need to ask you something. And don't tell me you haven't a dress. I had reports that the one you wore at the Muller estate will do very nicely.'

Fitzroy widened his grin and raised one eyebrow at me. 'I know you, Euphemia. You don't like me enough to come down for me,' he said, 'but you'll come because you might get to dance with your beloved Bertram –' I interrupted to protest, but Fitzroy continued, 'But mostly you'll come because you're bored stupid and I can offer you a little adventure.'

Our eyes locked. I held his gaze for a good minute before I sighed. 'Oh, all right.'

'Good.' Fitzroy made to enter my room. I placed my hand on his chest.

'You can wait out there.'

'Spoilsport,' said Fitzroy, but he stayed outside rudely, if tunefully, whistling while I scrambled into my dress and brushed out my hair.

I had never seen the ballroom opened up in all my time at Stapleford Hall. Large, airy, lined with mirrors, and edged with a minstrels' gallery, it lay on the eastern-most edge of the south wing. Silk wallpaper the colour of champagne lined the walls and on tables all along one of the shorter sides there were servants tending to buckets of the real thing. Music played loudly for the colourful throng that merged before my eyes and I smelt the sweat of a hundred people who had been enjoying a good dance.

As I entered the ballroom on Fitzroy's arm we attracted no little attention. Fortunately guests were no longer being announced, but by pausing a moment at the threshold somehow Fitzroy managed to get quite a few sets of eyes turning our way. I knew my dress suited me and I also knew that with the exception of Bertram and Richenda no one else in the room would recognise me. Fitzroy appearing with a mysterious and attractive lady on his arm when no further carriages were due to arrive was as close to a public scandal as I had ever caused. I saw Bertram's face in the crowd below, scowling fiercely.

Fitzroy must have seen him too as he led me over and handed me on to Bertram as the musicians struck up an old-fashioned waltz. Fortunately my mother had ensured I could dance. Bertram's mother had obviously not placed quite so much importance on the skill. Although I admit that with the strange feeling of Bertram's hands on me I was not as graceful as my mother would have expected.

'What the devil are you doing here,' hissed Bertram in my ear.

'You have not mastered the art of polite conversation with your dancing partner, have you?' I teased. Bertram's scowl deepened further, if that were possible, and his face began to turn red. I noticed with a shock he was sporting large sideburns. 'You're not thinking of growing a beard, are you?' I said, horrified.

'Why not?' snapped Bertram. 'It will give me gravitas.'

'Who on earth told you that?' I said in genuine surprise.

'Never mind that,' said Bertram turning a deeper shade of red, 'what the devil do you mean coming down to the ball when you know it will only enrage Richard? He could turn you out!'

'I doubt that. He doesn't want to upset Richenda. Besides, have you ever tried to say no to Fitzroy?'

'So that's what he meant!' growled Bertram stepping hard on my foot. 'Well, I'm not having it!'

'Having what?'

'He's got something he wants me to do for the security of the nation or some such tosh. When I resisted his plan he said if I knew who else was involved I might change my mind. Then he disappeared until he brought you in.'

My heart beat faster and I had a strange sensation of bubbling in my chest. Both Bertram and I had had to sign the Official Secrets Act so it was possible that Fitzroy might ask us do something secretive. Nothing too dangerous, I suspected, as both of us were in his eyes ordinary civilians.

'Did he say what?'

'No,' said Bertram shortly.

'Whatever it is it's got to be better than staying here.'

'You might get shot!' said Bertram, referring to events in my journal *A Death in the Highlands*.

'As I recall it was Fitzroy who prevented me getting shot!'

'And McLeod. He wants him in on it too. He's back, you know.' Bertram swung me inexpertly round and my eyes locked with the Stapleford butler, Rory McLeod, the man I had once thought was the love of my life till he jilted me. He stood behind the waiting tables, sharp in his uniform, glowering at the sight of me in Bertram's arms.

It seemed as if life was about to become interesting again. Well, I had asked for it, hadn't I?

Chapter Five:

The wild country or will ye go lassie, go?

It was three o'clock in the morning before Fitzroy gathered
Bertram, Rory, and myself in one room to have his little
chat. He had chosen, whether through prior knowledge or
pure chance, the place where I had found my first dead
body at Stapleford Hall, the library. Rory stood ramrod-
straight by the window, only the shadows under his eyes
showing how exhausted he was. Bertram ambled round the
room until he came to rest leaning heavily against the
mantelpiece, his coat tails hanging dangerously near the
fire. I guessed he was less than sober. No longer a servant,
I chose to sit in the wing-backed chair near the fire.
Fitzroy sauntered in with not a hair out of place, looking as
if he had spent the last eight hours in a restful sleep and
not dancing non-stop in the ballroom. He took a long,
theatrical look around at the three of us. 'Definitely a few
cobwebs that need dusting away,' he said obscurely. Then
he closed the door behind him, checked that the door to the
servants' passage behind the bookcase was firmly closed
(and no, I don't know how he knew it was there), and
began his speech.

'I'll be brief,' he said, 'there is a very important
meeting that needs to be held in the Highlands. A small
group of men discussing an issue of national security in
these days of heightened tensions. My job is to put them

into a secure but obscure location. Richard Stapleford is lending the government his Highland Lodge and I require ...' Bertram and I both shot him a venomous look. Fitzroy bowed slightly. 'I should say, I *would like*, you to head up the staff and welcoming party there. All of you have experience in observation and in managing staff. You are discreet, have each signed the Official Secrets Act, and are personally known to me. While I would hope you were able to offer reports on the meeting after it has closed, I can say with certainty that at no time would any of you be in any physical danger. The government simply requires a discreet place where interested parties can discuss certain matters and where we can ensure that these matters are not reported in the press or picked up by the local people.'

'What matters would those be?' asked Rory, his Scotch accent more in evidence than usual.

Fitzroy straightened one of his cufflinks. 'I am afraid I am not at liberty to say.'

'And yet you want us to report on how matters progress?' continued Rory.

Fitzroy waved a dismissive hand. 'I need only to know how the various parties relate to each other. That will tell me all.' He looked at us all quickly in turn. 'Need I say I do trust you all implicitly.'

'But nae implicitly enough to tell us what is going on,' said Rory, becoming even more Scotch in his speech.

'Do we have a choice?' asked Bertram. He sounded resigned.

'Of course,' said Fitzroy, 'you are private citizens. If you choose to turn your back on your King and country when they need you then that is matter entirely between you and your conscience.'

'So no,' said Bertram.

'I will ensure that travel arrangements are made for

you. Expect to be collected on January 4th. There will be no need to arrange supplies I will sort all that. When you arrive at the lodge you, Bertram, will find a letter introducing you to your guests, who will arrive on the 6th.'

'How am I to explain this to Richenda?' I asked. 'You surely don't expect her to attend?'

'Matters will be arranged,' said Fitzroy. 'Now I must leave you. Happy New Year.' And with that he exited.

'Good Gad,' said Bertram, 'if I didn't know he was an employee of the King I'd think he was a – a –' He looked at me and hastily shut his mouth.

'Reckon he is that,' said Rory. 'If you will excuse me, sir and miss, I have the New Year breakfast to attend to. It will be served at 4 a.m. in the ballroom just prior to carriages arriving.'

'I need a drink,' said Bertram.

I said nothing, but made my way quietly to my bedroom. As I undressed for bed my head was awhirl with thoughts. I could hear the music and laughing as the ball spun on into the night, but even the possibility of an early breakfast could not tempt me to further wakefulness. I was to be sequestered with both Rory and Bertram in the heart of the lonely Highlands at a place where … it was too much to recall at this time of night. I tumbled into bed and pulled the covers over my head, but whether I was attempting to shut out the noises of the ball or the coming of the morrow I could not have said.

Chapter Six:

A nasty surprise from a man with a dubious sense of humour

New Year's Day itself saw the groaning, moaning house guests exit in a variety of states. Of the host himself there was no sign. Gilbert along with Rory saw people off the premises. Mrs Lewis did not step above stairs until the last party-goer had left. Richenda declared herself 'dying' and called on Merry to tend to her last breath. I learned about this from Merry herself when she unceremoniously dumped a breakfast tray in my room. 'Mrs Lewis said how you hadn't stayed up all night, unlike some of us, and I was to bring your breakfast.'

'That was very kind of her.'

'And bleeding Richenda has me dancing attendance on her because she's got the hangover from hell. I've been up all bleeding night and I'm ready to drop.'

'Do we have any sleeping powders in the house?'

'Probably. Why?'

'Bring me one and I will give it to Richenda. Then you can catch up on some sleep while you watch her.'

'Blimey, you've changed haven't you? You're happy to drug your employer?'

'The best thing when someone has taken too much quantity of drink is for them to sleep,' I said pointedly. 'I thought I was doing you both a favour.'

'Yeah, well, I suppose,' said Merry. She sniffed. 'It's not like I'm not grateful. It's just going to be a bit odd. That's all.'

'What is?'

'Apparently I'm being sent up into the Highlands to help you out. That's what Mr Bertram just told me.'

'He's up, is he?' I asked, sidestepping the elephant in the room. Merry and I had worked side by side and while bringing (and sharing) the odd meal with me at Stapleford House didn't tax her dignity too much, it would be strange for both of us to be in a house for an extended time where she was below stairs and I was above.

'I think he expects me to be your bleedin' maid.'

I was aware of Merry's long-held ambition to rise to the position of a lady's maid, but I don't think she had had me in mind. 'I'm sure it's just to preserve the proprieties,' I said soothingly. 'I hear it is to be an entirely male party other than myself.'

'Richenda's not going?' asked Merry.

I was spared the answer by the very person we were discussing erupting through my bedroom door. 'Hans has sent for me!' she cried, waving a telegram in our faces, 'I am to join him and his cousin in a visit to a most excellent German spa!'

'Oh,' I said, wondering how Fitzroy was going to get around this. 'How soon?'

'I travel tomorrow!' She came across and pressed a hot hand on mine. 'I am sorry, Euphemia, but Hans and his cousin are coming to collect me tomorrow. His cousin will be acting as chaperone.' She paused. Then looked meaningfully at me. 'Your services will not be required.'

'Ever again,' I gasped.

'Oh good gracious me, I didn't mean that,' said Richenda, posing languidly against a wall. 'No, apparently this woman wishes to be my maid of honour – it's complicated. Hans doesn't explain it that well here. But as soon as I'm back on British soil I will need you again.'

I breathed a sigh of relief.

'But what will you do until I return? Richard will not want to house you indefinitely?'

'I will manage,' I said, thinking I should never have doubted Fitzroy. 'I'm glad to see you up and about, Richenda. Merry feared you were very ill.'

'I was feeling a little unwell,' confessed Richenda, 'but Hans's news has bucked me up considerably.'

She made a little hiccoughing noise and then threw up violently all over my bedroom rug. She had the grace to blush and exit quickly from the room.

'I'll get a bucket and a scrubbing brush, shall I?' said Merry, obviously not best pleased.

I surveyed the hideous mess. 'Burn it,' I said shortly. 'If you wouldn't mind taking my breakfast tray away, Merry. I think you'd better bring up that medicine for Richenda we were discussing. I'll be in the library.' Merry's expression made it quite plain what she thought of the fact I got to leave her to clean up the mess, but she nodded curtly in agreement.

The next few days of 1912 passed quietly. It was on the fourth I found myself sitting in a carriage with Bertram as the train chugged forward to the high hills of Scotland. 'I am not at all sure this is proper,' he protested for the hundredth time.

'Would you rather I travelled third class with Merry and Rory?'

'No, of course not,' said Bertram tugging on his growing beard. 'What on earth was Fitzroy thinking sending you up there unchaperoned?'

'Who chaperones the chaperone?' I said lightly.

'It's not a laughing matter, Euphemia. Reputation!'

'I'm sure yours will survive it.'

'You know that's not what I meant!' snapped Bertram. Then he jumped to his feet. 'I almost forgot, Fitzroy handed me this for you.' He pulled down one of his briefcases from the luggage rack.

'I did wonder why you had two.' Bertram passed it to me and took down the other. He opened his. 'Papers,' he said in disgust. 'He must expect me to read this lot on the way up.'

I barely registered his words. I was staring down horrified at the contents of my case. 'He cannot be serious,' I said.

There must have been something about my tone for I swear for a moment Bertram looked somewhat afraid. 'What?' he asked, tugging again on his beard. I feared this was going to become a new and extremely annoying habit.

In answer to him I held up the contents of the briefcase.

'A maid's outfit!' exclaimed Bertram.

'There is a note attached,' I said coldly. I read in silence, while Bertram attacked his facial hair once more. 'It seems that Fitzroy does share your moral misgivings after all. He writes the only way to have me at the lodge without a chaperone is for me to go in disguise as a maid. He has the effrontery to add that this will also enable me to see another side of the negotiations.'

'How the hell do we explain this to Merry?' asked Bertram.

'Or Susan,' I said darkly, referring to the woman who had been 'local help' when I was at the Highland Lodge.

'Richard made her permanent housekeeper,' said Bertram.

'Wonderful,' I said. 'This little jaunt just gets better and better.'

'Would you like to play chess to pass the time?' said Bertram timidly, 'I brought a travelling set.'

'Certainly,' I said, gritting my teeth. I then proceeded to thrash him game after game until we arrived at our destination. Bertram had the sense not to complain.

Chapter Seven:

A return to old haunts

I changed in the ladies' restroom at the station. Then without explanation climbed into the servant's cart in my maid's outfit. Merry's eyes grew wide as saucers, but something about my demeanour advised her not to ask questions – yet. Rory scowled at me ferociously as if he thought I was playing some deliberate trick to annoy him. I turned my back. The cart began its long, uncomfortable drive across the wretchedly bad Scotch roads as the day slid into a purple dusk that in different circumstances I might have appreciated.

We arrived after much bumping and shuggling at the servants' entrance to Lord Stapleford's lodge. By this time, Merry, always a poor traveller, was fit for nothing more than her bed. It was left to Rory and me to unload. We entered through the servants' entrance. I sent Merry straight upstairs, presuming that we had been put in the room we had shared before.

As we made our way through the labyrinth of servants' passages we heard the familiar cursing of Jock the chef as he wrangled with the old cooking range. Bertram's trunks had gone on ahead with him. I had no idea how he had had them taken up to his room, but as protocol dictated we left our bags backstairs and went to meet the housekeeper. We were, after all, invading her domain.

I was not looking forward to this meeting. Susan Simpson, the widowed maid with whom I had such a difficult relationship, due it is only fair to say to the interference of various men, was now housekeeper at the Lodge.[2]

'Oh, how the mighty are fallen!' Susan stood with her hands on her hips and stared at me. She looked much better than when I had last seen her. There was colour in her face and her frame was no longer thin from lack of nutrition – on her previously small salary she had been forced to choose between feeding herself or her children.

'I – er – um,' I began. I looked up hopefully at Rory, but the gaze he returned to me was impassive and cold. 'I hope …' I began, when Susan rushed over to me and threw her arms around my neck.

'Away with yer, yer silly bissum!' she said, 'it's thanks to you I'm housekeeper here. I tell you it's the grandest place to work for the Staplefords. They never come near or by the place.'

I felt myself relax. Tiredness swept over me and tears pricked my eyes. 'It's good to see you doing so well,' I managed to say. My throat was sore with emotion. Rory's cold impersonal attitude was taking its toll on me.

'Was there not another maid coming with you? We've got a right houseful coming by all reckoning. Might even need a lady's maid.'

---

[2] I confess I often feel if only men would stay longer in the smoking room we could all get on with things so very much more effectively. There would also be much more taking of tea and the place would be generally tidier, men being in both their persons and about themselves generally untidy. Take Bertram's beard, for instance. Actually, please take Bertram's beard. It is ghastly!

'Really?' I said surprised. 'Merry's with us, but she travels so badly she's gone straight to bed. She'll be good for nothing until the morning.'

'Come sit yourselves down,' said Susan pointing us to the big kitchen table. 'You must be guy starving. Jock's cooked up some guid stuff to stick to your ribs. Goodness knows yous is going to be worked off your feet the next few days.'

'If you don't mind, Mrs Simpson, I will take my repast in the butler's pantry,' said Rory.

The Susan I had known would have told him what she thought of his standoffishness, but this version had obviously grown with her job. 'Certainly, Mr McLeod,' she said, 'I will have our footman bring it to you.' Rory nodded curtly and left.

'What's up with the stuffed shirt?' she asked me when he'd gone. 'I always thought you two would make a go of it.'

For a moment I considered blurting out the full story, but all I said was, 'I have no idea.' Susan gave me a long look that said she saw right through me. Then she passed on the plate Jock handed to her. 'Get yourself around them tatties and sausages, hen.'

The next morning came and went in a flurry of dusting, cleaning, and making up the bedrooms. Susan would have mucked in with us, but Rory called her away to sort through menus and other matters 'more suited to her station', as he put it. Merry had yet to comment on my sudden demotion. I think she was simply glad she had help. Whoever was coming to this meeting, the actual numbers had only been given to Susan yesterday.

Merry, Susan, and myself were finishing a fine early lunch. The male servants were eating elsewhere. Suddenly

47

the doorbell rang.

'Oh Lord, they're early,' said Susan. She stood up, straightening her skirt.

Rory appeared in the doorway. 'I looked for you in the housekeeper's room,' he said coldly. 'Come now. The guests must not ring twice.' He said this as if it meant the world would end. Merry and I also rose, but he shook his head.

'Too lowly to be seen,' said Merry when they'd gone. She sat down again with a shrug. 'Pass those flat floury things, will you, Euphemia.'

'Potato scones,' I said sadly.

'Hmm,' said Merry, 'whatever they are they're very tasty. I'm still hungry from …'

'No details please, Merry. I saw enough of your suffering on the cart.'

'I've been meaning to ask –' began Merry, when Susan burst through the door.

'The whole lot of 'em have arrived at once and they want luncheon in half an hour! Girls, you're going to have to help serve.'

'Who are they?' I asked.

'There's a Miss Flowers, who you can tell is going to be trouble, and the Mr Smiths.' Then she was off again to check on the dining room.

'Did she say the Smiths as in more than one?' asked Merry.

I achieved a creditable shrug despite my mother's training. 'No idea. Jock, what do you need doing?' I asked.

Merry was given the task of taking in the soup tureen. Rory would serve from it, but Merry had to hold it level. I was to precede them with a selection of rolls. Merry was frankly terrified. The tureen was old, expensive-looking, and very heavy. I curbed the thought that it had been given to the tinier Merry because Rory didn't want to stand next to me. Fortunately there was a dumb waiter, so the tureen was winched up while we maids pelted up the stairs. Rory was already in situ in the dining room.

Around the table sat six men and one woman.[3] Bertram sat at one end of the table. He was thoughtfully scratching his beard, but stopped when he felt my eyes on him. Goodness knew how he was going to manage with the soup.

At the other end of the table sat a middle-aged man in a well-tailored discreet dark suit. Everything from his neat blond hair to his clean fingernails was smartly average. I guessed this must be the representative in charge of the meeting.[4] On his right sat a female, her hair so bright in colour I had trouble believing it was natural. Despite the early hour the ruddiness of her cheeks was also false and she had a sparkling necklace around her neck. Even if it was real, it was definitely not the time of day for such a thing. She was, as Merry would later put it, 'no better than she ought to be'. My mother would simply have sniffed and snubbed her. I, on the other hand, offered her the rolls. She paid no attention to me as she took one of the larger ones. Her hand hovered over the tray for a second. A glance around the table and she withdrew it. Greedy too, I thought.

The other four diners were all men in suits. None of them were in the least flamboyant. The woman among

---

[3] The more perceptive of you will note I do not refer to her as a lady.

[4] I use the term 'representative' because I had no idea who he represented, simply that he was one of the discreet fellows who worked for King and Country in capacities that generally bypassed lesser mortals such as myself.

49

them stood out like a parrot in a field of sheep. The atmosphere in the room was strangely tense. The woman and the man in charge seemed relaxed enough, but the five men, including Bertram, were all sitting on the edges of their seats. Bertram's face had the bemused, worried expression I had so often seen when workmen came to tell him yet again that another part of his cursed estate had been found to be falling down again. I suspected he felt out of his depth and somewhat lost, like the rest of us, at what was actually going on. At least I had something to do. Merry's arms, I noted with alarm, were beginning to shake with effort, so when the footman appeared I tried to catch his eye to get him to take over from her. He ignored me – as footmen usually do with maids, above stairs, and tried to whisper in Rory's ear, but Rory's furious face made him back off immediately. Rory set the ladle down in the soup. He tapped me on the shoulder, gesturing that I should take over and left with the footman. I placed the roll tray on the buffet and ignoring Rory's suggestion took the soup tureen from Merry. She gave me a silent look of gratitude. I flicked my eyes at the woman, but Merry served the man at the top of the table first, only spilling a few drops on the tablecloth. Bertram coughed and she immediately realised her faux pas. The woman, however she looked, should have been served first.

'So sorry,' Merry muttered under her breath and in a shaking hand lifted the ladle once more. She managed to lift it without shaking too badly when Rory walked back into the room. Merry, startled mid-serve, emptied her ladle neatly into the lap of the woman, who shot to her feet with a screech.[5] Rory's flaming eyes met mine. It was clear he thought it was all my fault.

---

[5] And she did sound akin to a parrot!

The man at the head of the table began to dab ineffectually at the woman's lap area with his napkin, which made her screech even louder, like a kettle on the boil. She knocked his hand brusquely away and rushed for the door, pushing past Merry and I. On the way she caught Merry by the shoulder and sent her flying. I only retained hold of the soup tureen by a supreme effort of will and by planting my feet in a most unladylike pose. Poor Merry ended up on the buffet, rolls flew everywhere, and we were treated to a distinct flash of Merry's underwear. Bertram's eyes grew wide as saucers and one of the other men stifled, none too effectively, a guffaw. Poor Merry scrambled to her feet and fled.

Chapter Eight:

Messages (too many of 'em)

Of course, Rory handled the situation in cool, professional manner. He put the rolls tray in the dumb waiter, hopefully signalling to the kitchen below he needed a new stock. Retrieving the ladle, he polished it on a napkin from the buffet, glided over to Bertram, and said smoothly, 'Soup, Mr Stapleford?' Realising I still had the tureen I staggered over, so that by the time he lowered his ladle there was something to immerse it in. Bertram, scratching furiously at his beard, made a little bleating noise which Rory liberally interpreted as a yes and filled his soup bowl with a flourish.

The meal continued. The woman did not return and while I was in the room at least the conversation was muted, consisting of such comments as: 'A fine soup, Stapleford' or 'Well-seasoned sauce, this'. No one of course referred to the incident. I felt a momentary nostalgic pang for the Stapleford House retinue, who were uncivilised enough to discuss murder over lunch and would certainly have commented on Merry's display. Here everything hung heavily unsaid in the air. Everyone was oppressively civil. My mother would have been proud of them, but I fear my standards had been lowered and I would have been glad of hearing everything that shouldn't be said in front of the servants. Bertram was a sad storyteller and I knew would make a fearful mess of explaining what was eventually said over the cigars.

I kept up my appearance of professional disinterest. Inside I was longing to get away to see Merry, but no footman appeared to relieve me. Instead Rory and I served the entire meal, barely looking at each other. It was agonising. I knew enough of Merry to know she would be throwing a fair fit downstairs. I also had no idea where the footman had gone, and if my life has taught me anything it is these little mysteries that often reveal the whole. I barely spared a thought for the be-souped woman. I felt she had got no more than she deserved, dressed the way she had been for luncheon!

Finally everything that could be served was served. Rory would have to stay on hand, but I loaded the final serving dishes in the dumb waiter and nodded to Rory indicating I was leaving. I didn't wait for any response, but closed the door quietly behind me before flying down the servants stairs.

I found Susan sitting in the kitchen with a very large mug of tea in front of her. Jock was banging and clattering about the range and muttering even louder and even more unintelligibly than usual.

'Whit do you ken about being a lady's maid, Euphemia?'

'Not a lot,' I said sitting down. Jock slammed a cup of tea, unasked, in front of me. At least I think it was tea. It was darker than pitch and when I added a little milk from the jug on the table it still appeared unable to reflect light.

'Nothing?' asked Susan again.

'It was always more Merry's thing than mine.' I paused. 'Do you we have a lady coming to stay?'

'Pah!' said Susan and Jock almost simultaneously.

'Miss Flowers wants someone to get the soup out of her

skirt and to do her hair for this evening.'

'Does she? I don't think you'll find Merry offering after what happened upstairs.'

'Miss Flowers wants her dismissed!'

'What!' I cried, outraged.

'Euphemia, I've not long been a housekeeper, but even I'm aware that the dumping of soup in a lady's lap is grounds for dismissal.'

I knew she was right and cursed Rory for his refusal to let me carry the tureen. 'Have you given her her letters?' I asked, referring to the practise of given a reference to an outgoing servant.

'Thankfully,' said Susan, 'she is not a member of my staff. It will be up to Mr McLeod and Mr Stapleford to decide what to do. Personally I think whoever decided a tiny maid unused to serving should deal with that great cauldron of soup pot is a gormless eejit!'

Not all the words were familiar to me, but I agreed with the sentiment. 'What happened to your footman?' I asked.

'Postie called to say his mother had taken a turn for the worse and they'd called in the priest. She lives down in the village. Scott, that's the footman, is the apple of his mother's eye, so he's away to her side.'

'We're going to be very short staffed,' I said.

'I rather think he told Mr McLeod he was going rather than asked.'

I shook my head. 'Of course he should have gone, but with Merry – out of the picture for now – at least, there's only the three of us plus Jock.'

Jock banged down a pot and turned and shot something at me that I couldn't make head nor tail of.

Susan gave a faint smile. 'He says there's no enough money in the world that could get him working above stairs among the loons.'

I nodded at Jock. 'Believe me,' I said earnestly, 'I completely understand.'

Susan gave me a shrewd look. 'There's something funny going on here, isn't there? It's bad enough four of 'em gave their names as Smith even though they're not related…'

'They're all called Smith?'

Susan nodded, 'Except yon high hied'jin who told me to call him sir.'

'Blimey,' I said borrowing from Merry's vocabulary. 'That must be the man from the ministry.'

'Mr Ministry, is it?' said Susan, who was deep in her own thoughts and not really listening to me. 'There's some kind of shady plot afoot, isn't there? Not that I care. The worst thing to my mind is Mr Stapleford's beard. Fair gives me the shivers that.'

'I know,' I said sadly, 'that a handsome man could make himself look so badly.'

'They'll be a woman behind it,' said Susan. 'You mark my words.'

At this point I made my exit. I wanted time to talk with Bertram and Merry. I also wanted to be out of range for any more of Susan's questions.

Merry was defiant, but scared. At Susan's request she was staying in her room until Rory made his decision. I tried to reassure that her long history with the Stapleford family would stand her in good stead, but she argued every one of my points down as if was determined to head into tragedy. It was clear she was far too prickly to be otherwise consoled, so I would be better leaving her be.

I was literally wondering where to put myself, not in my room (with Merry), not in the kitchen (with questioning Susan) and not in any part of the house where I might run into the guests. I had come down to considering the stables, when I heard a 'psst'. Bertram's face appeared round the door of the small library. I immediately pushed the door open. Bertram staggered back.

'Careful Euphemia,' he said, 'one of us ending up arse over apex is enough for today.' He gave a broad grin.

'It's not funny,' I snapped. 'The wretched woman wants Merry sacked.'

'Well, that's not going to happen,' said Bertram to my great relief. 'Girl's a tart.' He gave his beard a frantic scratch. 'Saving your presence.'

'Not quite the words I would have used,' I said, helping myself to a small sherry and pouring him a whisky. 'But I agree with the sentiment.'

Bertram boggled at me with the glasses for a moment then shut the door. 'I'm used to acting as a companion now,' I said stiffly, 'not as a servant.'

'Well, yes, I know, but we're undercover and all that.'

I sat down in one of the library's wing-backed chairs and sipped my sherry. 'Have you any idea what is going on?'

'They've got a lot of maps of Scotland,' said Bertram. 'I caught one of them poring over a set in here just before luncheon. He scrunched them all up at once when he heard the door open. Terrible way to treat 'em. Mind you when he saw it was me he seemed to relax a bit.'

'And they're all called Smith?'

'Incredible co-incidence,' agreed Bertram.

I gave him a long look.

Bertram sank down in the other chair. 'You mean they're using aliases?'

Now, I don't want you to think for a moment that Bertram is deficient in cerebral material, but while it once seemed I was the less world-aware of the two of us, and in some ways I suspect I still am, the past few years have worn away my natural inclination to believe people are telling the truth. It seemed this had not happened to Bertram.

He slapped his hand hard on his forehead. 'I'm an idiot,' he said. I didn't contradict him. 'The other chap is definitely a ministry man and has completely avoided giving his name.'

'He's from the church?' I asked confused.

'The government.'

'Which department then?'

'I don't think we're meant to know,' said Bertram. 'I'm increasingly sure that we don't have to do anything. Fitzroy really did just want people up here that he knew didn't have other loyalties or affiliations.'

'To what?'

'To whatever is relevant to whatever they're doing.'

'And servants who won't ask questions about their names.'

'Or peek through their papers,' said Bertram.

'You have stayed in some dubious houses, haven't you?' I said. 'No maid under my control would ever do such a thing.'

'That's because I pay a decent wage and when you were my housekeeper you were very fair with all the staff. Generally the richer the householder the more he begrudges paying his staff. The great houses still believe it's an honour to serve in them or even to be accosted by their lustful offspring.'

My face must have shown my shock. 'Sorry, Euphemia, I had a devil of a lot of wine at luncheon. Only way I could get through and now you've topped me up with whisky. I may spend the afternoon asleep in my room.'

'How very upper-class of you,' I said. Bertram winced. 'What are the rest of them doing?' I asked.

'That's the thing. They've asked Rory to turn the shooting room into a meeting room.'

'I hope he's locked up the guns,' I said forebodingly.

'Don't put ideas into my head, Euphemia,' said Bertram shivering. 'Anyway, outside of meals they will be holding meetings. My presence is not required and neither is yours.'

'So for once this could be not an adventure at all?' I said.

'Lord, let's hope,' said Bertram. His eyelids began to drop and it became clear our discussion was at an end. I turned over in my mind what I had learned and realised how very little it was. I didn't think the Smiths were from the government. My best guess was that they were some sort of contractor or supplier, who were bidding for a government project. Presumably one that was to take place in Scotland if Bertram was right about the maps. They only reason I could think of it being so secret was that once it was known it was going to be very unpopular, which would again be why Bertram hadn't been let in on the secret. Richard Stapleford MP definitely had interests in the arms business, and might have offered to lend the lodge to get back in the government's good books, but it obviously meant something that it had been his younger brother who had been chosen to play host. But what?

Miss Flowers I dismissed as a secretary with ideas above her station. She must also be foolish enough to believe she had a bullet-proof reputation if she was happy to reside in a small lodge in the middle of nowhere with her boss (presumably) *and* four other men. I judged the men to all be around middle age, and thus presumably at their height of their careers. It also meant they had all reached the age when men generally believe they have the right to do as they please.

I finished my sherry, relieved the sleeping Bertram of his glass – who else was there to tidy up? – and decided that after dropping off the glasses at the kitchen I would go for a bracing walk. I closed the door of the library quietly behind me, concentrating on letting it click only ever so slightly, so I would not wake Bertram, and so did not notice the man behind me.

He tapped me smartly on the shoulder and I jumped in the air and gave a little shriek. I heard a muffled 'What! What! What!' noise from Bertram and then a giant snore. Clearly he was to be of no help. I turned and faced my accoster, schooling my features to copy Mama's.[6] The little man shrunk back.

'Oh good heavens,' he said in a soft voice, 'I didn't mean to startle you, my dear. Allow me to introduce myself; I am Mr …'

'Smith,' I said trying to make the one word sound as cutting as possible.

The man gave a wry smile. 'Indeed,' he said. He was slightly below my height with narrow shoulders and weak blue eyes behind round moon glasses. His hair though cut short was a burnished gold and extremely thick. Many a debutante would have given if not her eyes then her servant's eyes for such a mane.

'I was wondering if you would do me the service of posting my letter.' He thrust a small, thick envelope at me that I took instinctively. 'It is most important that it is posted today and that no one else knows of its existence. Affairs of the heart,' he said and tapped the side of his

---

[6]My mother, a lady of 4'11", could make 6' footmen cry with a single harsh word when she was young.

nose. 'I'm sure a pretty young woman like yourself knows all about such things.'

The letter did indeed smell of cologne.

'Here's a few pennies,' said the blond man, tipping a few coins into my other hand. 'Just between us? I know I can trust you.' He gave his wry smile again and turned and walked off, displaying a very slight limp.

I stood looking down at the letter in my hand, a variety of conflicting thoughts running through my head. Rory appeared at the end of the corridor while I was still considering my options. I felt a flood of relief. I wouldn't need to take the decision alone. But as he came nearer I saw his expression was as foreboding as ever and without thinking I stuffed the letter into my apron pocket.

'Where is Mr Stapleford?' he demanded.

I indicated the library behind me. Rory made a superb *humph*ing sort of noise that I thought only butlers of considerable maturity were able to deliver. 'Have you nothing better to do than stand around here?' He scolded. 'If not, I noticed the rugs in the hall could do with a good beating.'

Chapter Nine:

A Highland walk proves most unsatisfactory

It would shortly be dusk. Unlike Merry, I have no fear of too many trees, but I was unfamiliar enough with the local countryside to wish not to be out after dusk. I also assumed, though Rory had not seen fit to tell me so, that he and I would be serving all the meals from now on. Susan might be housekeeper, but she had never served at table, and indeed in anything other than a Highland Lodge her training would be considered barely that of a 'tweenie maid. Of course, I had no intention of telling her this.

When I set out, with general directions from Susan for the main village where I would find a shop with a postal service, it was chilly but bright. However, I knew the Scotch weather all too well from my first visit and took a shawl with me to cover my head in case of rain. When you have as much hair as I do, being damp is not an option. After a walk through wet country lanes I am all too liable to smell akin to a wet dog.

Still I was away from all the stresses known and unknown at the Lodge and under a bright sky. I found myself whistling, a little tunelessly for music is not my talent, and walking with a skip in my step. The path Susan had set me on was barely a footpath at all. It wound between tall trees and skirted fields, some tamed, some still wild. I certainly did not need to be wary of passing carts. By my estimation I was about halfway to the village when I felt the hairs on the back of my neck prickle.

It is difficult to explain, but those of you who have had the feeling of being watched will know it only too well. It is like some primal animal instinct that warns you may now be prey. I became most aware of where I was putting my feet. I took the opportunity of bends in the path to look behind me, but despite my breathing becoming increasingly rapid I did my best not to show my alarm. It could be nothing more than a noisy village child curious about 'them from the big hoose'.

Had I done the right thing in not telling Rory or Bertram about the letter? Bertram would have wanted to open it, but my conscience could not allow that. We were not directly employees of Fitzroy and no one had yet suggested to me that prying into the guests' private affairs was why I was present at the Lodge. The letter did smell highly of men's cologne, and I had been inclined to think it was a billet-doux even if the gentleman who handed it to me was most unprepossessing. I knew the world well enough to know if he was rich there would be some women who would happily respond to his advances.

A twig snapped behind me. What if I had got this all entirely wrong and the letter was some secret government missive that I had been entrusted with? What if it contained … here my imagination faltered. It was not a large letter. Surely the diagrams for new armaments would take up more space than this? I had never seen any, but I imagined them to be quite complex.

Naturally, considering armaments led me quickly down the path of what people do with such things and I began to wonder if I was in serious danger. The skin down both of my arms prickled. It became harder and harder to curb my impulse to bolt. Somehow I knew if I ran I would be chased. The stark beauty of the countryside around me took on a sinister turn. I could no longer hear the birds calling. No cattle lowed nearby. I scanned the horizon. I could see no sign of the village. I could also see no one else on the path or even working in the field. Of course, at this time of year there was little to do with the frost-covered ground. But it suddenly seemed as if the silence was unnatural. As if everyone had felt the same foreboding and fled.

Time stretched into eternity. I knew each step took me closer to my doom. Another twig snapped behind me and I gave a little involuntary cry. I darted behind a tree and attempted to hide. The ridiculousness was not lost on me. Tree trunks are round and I had no idea on which side my enemy waited. I pressed my back against the tree and began to slowly skirt its circumference. Fields, scattered forest and scrubby hills met my eyes. A patch of low-lying foliage to my far left moved slightly. I held my breath. A rabbit, I told myself, maybe two. There was no dangerous wildlife here. Only humans, the most dangerous creatures of all. As I watched some leaves parted and I caught sight of an ugly misshapen claw bigger than my hand.

However good my imagination it could not have conjured that. I gave a full-throated scream and bolted. Heavy footsteps thudded behind me. I did not spare the time to look back. I ran on and on. My only hope was to reach the village. My heart thudded in my chest and perspiration ran in rivulets down my back. My feet thudded against the solid compacted earth until the soles were red and sore, but I did not stop. I fled for my life. The pins from my hair scattered and I didn't stop to pick them up. Sobs welled up in my chest. I thought of Rory. I thought of Bertram. I cursed Fitzroy. I arrived in the village looking like a madwoman.

A common well signified the beginning of the village. A few young women were loitering beside it chattering. As one they fell silent.

'A m-m-monster,' I stammered. 'A creature in the forest that has no right to be. An abomination.'

'I've heard Old Wifie Campbell called many things, but that's a new one on me,' laughed one young woman with a scarlet scarf covering her hair.

I sank down on the well steps. 'I'm serious,' I panted, 'there is something out there.'

The three girls regarded me with a mixture of amusement and pity. 'You be from the Lodge? One of them Londoners?' asked another. She had the dark rich red hair natural to the Scotch and violet eyes. Anywhere else she would have been accounted a beauty.

'From the Lodge, yes,' I managed to say. I was still catching my breath.

'That'll be it then,' said the third girl, who seemed to be their leader despite, or perhaps because of, the fine collection of moles she sported on her chin. 'Easy for them that doesn't know the countryside to get spooked.'

'I was brought up in the country,' I said. I fished around in my hair for remaining pins. I had an inkling of how I must look.

'So who are you then?' asked scarlet scarf not unkindly.

'I'm a –' I stumbled, what was I? 'A maid from the Lodge brought up for the party.'

'Aye, right,' jumped in the red-headed girl. 'One of them pinching jobs from the likes of us.'

'No,' I said weakly, though I knew they had every right to feel that way.

'Come on, girls,' said Moles, 'we've got work to do. Unlike some.' And they left me sitting there shaking on the well steps.

What I had taken as a pile of discarded clothing, shuffled up to me. 'I seen it too,' it hissed in a whisper redolent of rotting teeth and bad meat. 'It's a creature from hell. It's come to take the disbelievers away. Like the priest said.' Although the words were well-formed, the mouth that spoke them was slack on one side and spit foamed and ran down his chin. His head (I was fairly certain it was a man) was bald except for a strange translucent fuzz that stood out in the sunlight like a halo.

'I need to find the village shop,' I said.

'Won't do no good now the hell gates have opened,' said my new friend sadly, but he pointed down the small high street.

I got to my feet and somewhat unsteadily attempted to recover what dignity I had. Really, it was unlike me to be so spooked.

I found the shop, with simple and hearty local produce decked out in front of it. The display was small, but it was winter. I entered. The normality of the wooden floor boards beneath my feet and the faint smell of flour and candles particular to small shops calmed me. An old woman got up slowly from her stool behind the desk and came forward.

'Yes?' she said querulously.

I explained I had a letter to post. This lady might have shaky hands and fingers knotted with arthritis, but she hefted my letter in one hand and told me what the postage would be. She then confirmed the weight with a little scale. I commended her on her skill. She smiled, showing her last few teeth. 'Been doing this bairn, lassie, and crone,' she said.

'It must be interesting,' I said. 'People must tell you all sorts of stories.'

The old lady gave a cackle. 'Gossip, you mean.' Then she peered more closely at me, 'You're looking a might peely-wally. That old eejit Jamie's not been filling your head with his nonsense has here.'

'Is he the gates of hell fellow?' I asked.

'Never been right since his mother dropped him on his head as a wean. Both parents deid. God-fearing twa they were. Thought the devil had got into his heid. Told yon minister could put him aright. It's a nonsense. Poor laddie's got mince fae brains.'

'I suppose he did scare me,' I admitted. 'I got a little spooked in the woods. I thought I saw something – someone,' I corrected myself. I gave a little laugh. 'So silly of me.'

The old lady's face hardened. 'You mind and take care of yourself out there. There's a German spy in the woods. Several of the girls and their young men have seen him.'

'A German spy?' I echoed in alarm.

The old lady nodded. 'Looks funny by all accounts, and speaks guy odd. One of the foresters recognised it as German.'

'A forester?'

'Aye, his father was in the Royal Navy before he settled here and married a local girl. Told the lad all about his travels and the people he'd met. Sure it was a German, Connel was.'

'I'll be very careful,' I promised her. I left the shop with a lighter heart. I did not believe any forester, who had probably stirred no more than ten miles from his home village, could identify the German language. And as for mad Jamie, well, I'd been as foolish as him. My last visit to the Lodge had been cataclysmic. I had not acknowledged to myself how concerned I was on returning. I was also feeling guilty about not telling the others about the letter. I gave myself a mental shake and set off with a lighter heart back to the Lodge.

My companions on my return journey were squirrels and wood pigeons. I had a most pleasant walk back. I felt no eyes on my back. The sun gave me a display of red, orange and brilliant gold as it nestled down towards the horizon ending the day in a blaze of glory.

I opened the servant's door of the Lodge and walked straight into Rory.

'Where the devil have you been?' he demanded. 'I need you to help serve dinner.' He scowled fiercely at me and stomped off. I held on to the image of the sunset in my head and walked into the kitchen with my head held high.

Chapter Ten:

Real concerns that this may be becoming an adventure

Dinner passed uneventfully. The formerly soupy woman wore an inappropriately low gown and giggled far too much for a supposedly serious gathering. Rory was impassively professional. When I was dismissed from the room I found Merry in the kitchen washing up and singing. Jock, making himself a late-night sandwich, joined in with his usual incomprehensible nonsense. Merry turned on hearing my step. She danced away from the sink and embraced me with soapy arms.

'I ain't being let go. Mr Bertram said they can all go boil their heads as far as he is concerned.'

I embraced her back. 'That's very good news.'

Merry scowled slightly. 'Apparently I have to stay behind the green door on account of 'Er 'Ighness is still upset with me. So you and Susan are going to have to do all the tidying, cleaning, and bed-making upstairs.' She gave me an evil little grin. 'So sorry.'

'I bet you are,' I said smiling back. I hoped this would also mean we would have less problems shielding Merry from the truth that Rory, Bertram, and I were all up to something – even if we didn't know what it was yet.

Tomorrow would bring an early rising, and I had finished my chores, so I said my goodnights and left Merry and Jock to their work.

The little room upstairs that Merry and I shared was compact, but clean and of a higher standard than most maids enjoy. I had carried my small trunk up the servants' stair, bumping it off each step. We had been here for less than two days but this was the first chance I had had to sort out my things. My second uniform bore deep crush marks and I hung it up by the window. I set out my own brush. I had been borrowing Merry's till now and it didn't have the strength of bristles to tackle my hair, which had been whipped into a mess by the Highland wind. I sat on the bed in my nightgown and gradually worked my way through the tangled tresses. By the time I was finished Merry had still not come up to bed, but I was bone weary. I snuggled down under my blankets, said my prayers, and composed myself for sleep.

I woke in the dark. My second uniform fluttered as it hung against the draughty window. Next to me Merry snored. Moonlight seeped in between the curtains. I listened hard. Nothing. I felt completely awake as if I had been shocked out of sleep, but strangely I didn't feel alarmed. I lay still, listening. My heart beat steadily. I could only conclude that I must have been awoken by a noise my sleeping brain did not consider unusual.

I turned over and tried to get back to sleep, but sleep was as far away as the moon that shone down on me. I sighed. 'Merry,' I whispered. 'Merry?' My only response was a snore. I tried again a little louder. And then again. It became clear that short of taking her bodily by the shoulders and shaking her Merry was not going to be roused.

I got out of bed. There was no way I was going back to sleep without going to see what was or was not happening in the Lodge. I decided not to take a candle, but to trust in my knowledge of the Lodge and the moonlight.

The last time I had wandered through the dark at this Lodge on a previous and fraught visit I had been so careful and concerned about where I might or might not go. But having spent a year as a Lady's Companion I found it difficult to go back to the subservient ways of a maid.[7]

I headed straight for the centre of the house. All seemed in order. I knew Rory would have locked up the Lodge with great care. I climbed the main staircase as quietly as I could, listening out at every step. I was almost at the top when I smelt something. Perfume. Then I heard a low girlish giggle. I had heard nothing more than the usual goings-on that occur on a weekly basis in the best houses in the land. No wonder I hadn't been frightened by the sound that awoke me. Could anything be more innocuous? And immoral …

That Miss Flowers's morals were lower than her décolletage did not surprise me. That any of the men at the Lodge would fall for such a woman surprised me. A serious meeting was taking place and someone was – and then it struck me. Miss Flowers would have access to not only all the notes from the meetings, but also whatever other papers the government man had brought with him. Could someone be using the silly girl to get an inside advantage on whatever deal was under discussion?

What if the letter had not been a silly love note, but papers of importance disguised by overpowering male cologne. Had I been played for a fool?

My heart plummeted. I might already have let something vital slip through my fingers because of my personal integrity. I mentally cursed Fitzroy. I knew he only interested himself in things that concerned affairs of

---

[7] To be honest, I had never been that subservient.

the nation. Usually our nation in relation to others. He would have had no qualms in opening the letter, reading it and resealing it. Or even confronting the sender.

The latter was clearly not my role, but the giggling was something he would expect me to investigate and report back to him on. Or rather he would want to know who was conducting themselves with less than the proper discretion. Another giggle floated through the air. I had to follow it. I took a deep breath and for once hoped my late father, the Rev. Martins, was not watching over me. I continued to ascend the stairs.

I reached the landing in ten swift steps. The floorboards creaked alarmingly under my feet. The latest giggle was cut off mid-stream. Instinctively I slipped into the shadow of the large curtained window. I held my breath and waited. Unfortunate thoughts ran through my mind.

I strained my ears, but I could hear no worried whispered conversation. I was too far away to hear. Dare I brave creeping along the upstairs passageway? I would in all likelihood be able to pinpoint whose bedroom the noises were emanating from. Every fibre of my being revolted. I waited several more heartbeats in the hope Miss Flowers would send her beau to check if anyone was on the prowl. I felt safe in the folds of my curtain. I could spy who it was and then go back to bed.

No one came. I would have to investigate. I left the safety of the curtains and began to make my way along the eastern corridor. There was little cover to conceal myself should someone hear me and come to challenge me, but the gas lamps were on their lowest setting. There were certainly some shadows darker than others and it was between these that I attempted to dodge.

After the moonlit staircase my eyes were having trouble adjusting to the dark. I held my head cocked on one side as I attempted to listen at the bedroom doors. I felt a sudden sharp pain in my shins and a fluttering of something fell about my face. I put up my arms to protect myself and soon found myself intertwined with a large aspidistra. I managed to steady the stand with my foot and after a brief impromptu waltz with the giant leafy thing I got it back on its pedestal. Once it was back in position the loudest sound was my breathing.

The thought of how Merry would have reacted to this silly scene made laughter bubble up inside me. The more I tried to suppress the more the chuckles pushed at me from within. I was becoming hysterical. I dug my nails into my palm until I felt wet beneath them. I scolded myself internally, 'this really will not do', but I sounded so like my mother in my own head that I was forced to stuff my fist into my mouth to stop any sound escaping.

I crouched beside the plant and tried to pull myself together. The giggling began again. No one had heard me. Considering it was a happy sound the noise sobered me. It came from one of three doors ahead. I could hear the low voice of a man murmuring now too. I felt myself flush as embarrassment washed over me. Though it is fair to say the couple I could hear should have been the ones feeling embarrassed. I needed to get closer to establish whose bedroom it was. I hadn't been involved in their allocation, but once I knew which room the liaison was taking place within I felt sure I could discover its occupier discreetly tomorrow. My plan would fail only if Miss Flowers' lover had gone to her room.

My family had kept some livestock so I was not wholly without knowledge of what the man and woman were indulging in in that bedroom. But being so close was painfully awful. I needed to get it over with quickly. I stood up from my hiding place.

As I did so one of the three doors opened. Like a rabbit retreating down a hole I crouched at once. A figure came out. I could tell it was a man by the silhouette. He checked up and down the corridor. Then pulled the door quietly behind him. With a brisk confident stride he glided quietly past me to the staircase. He did not see me as he passed the plant stand, but I saw him. It was Rory.

Shock rooted me to the spot. Of all the clandestine lovers I could have imagined, Rory had never figured among them. But then he had recently returned from butlering for an Earl of a great house, where doubtless liaisons among the guests were common. Perhaps it had gone further. Rory is extremely handsome, but I had thought better of him.

From being near hysterical with laughter, I now found silent tears were streaming down my face. Had I ever been so disappointed in a fellow human being? It wasn't even as if she was pretty. Let alone intelligent or having a modicum of breeding. Just the type, I thought depressingly, to seek a liaison with a handsome male servant. But Rory! How could he?

I slunk back along the corridor and made my way back down the main stairs. If I had found Rory would I have confronted him? I honestly don't know. I know hindsight is a poisonously insidious thing, but if I had taken the path to the butler's pantry and demanded to know what was going on right then it is more than likely a lot of what later came to pass would never have taken place.

But instead I pathetically and sadly fled to my bed. The moment I closed the door behind me the room was flooded with light. Mussy-haired but furious, Merry sat up in bed and demanded to know what was going on.

So I told her.

Chapter Eleven:

It all gets worse (as it always does)

'Rory? Doing the dirty with that woman? I don't believe it!'

I had, of course, limited my story to my night-time wanderings. It pained me greatly not to tell my best friend of the government's involvement in the Lodge party, but Fitzroy had been at pains to stress the severity of the repercussions should I break the Official Secrets Act. Though, on reflection, I can't recall him ever saying exactly what they were other than dire. Much as I loved Merry, I also knew she kept secrets about as well as a bootboy could be relied upon to guard sweets. They might set out with the best of intentions, but it would all go horribly (and in the case of the bootboy stickily) wrong.

'Are you sure that aspidistra didn't hit you on the head?' she asked. She paused to consider. 'I'd quite been enjoying the story of the waltz with the pot plant and vicar's daughter crouching outside the bedroom where two people were doing the naughty. But it all turns horrible and real once I know Rory's involved.'

'I had thought better of him.'

'I'd thought better of you, sneaking around like a peeping Tom!'

'I told you, I was investigating a noise. I thought it was a burglar.'

Merry gave me a withering look. 'A giggling burglar?'

'I know! I know!' I said desperately. And then, because there were so many questions I didn't want her to ask, I told her about my adventures in the forest.

When I finished Merry shivered dramatically. 'Now what did you have to go telling me that for? I'll not get a wink of sleep.'

'I don't think it is a German spy,' I said seriously. 'I think it's only a passing tramp.'

'I don't care about no German spy,' said Merry indignantly. 'The daft bugger you met, Jimmy? Or whatever he was called. I bet he was right. Them simple folk know a thing or two. That's what my mam always said. They see things others don't.' She tapped the side of her nose. 'He'd be the one who knew about the monster first and no one will listen to him. We'll all be murdered in our beds.' She let out a little shriek and dived head first under the covers.

'Oh come on, Merry,' I said in my sternest voice. 'Even you can't be that silly as to believe the ramblings of a village idiot.'

Merry's head appeared from under the covers. She was scowling. 'What do you mean, even me?'

'Besides, as the one formerly engaged to our philandering butler, I should be the one in a mess.'

Merry didn't miss a beat as I twisted the story on her. 'That's it!' she cried. 'It's all in your imagination. You only thought you saw Rory.'

'I can assure you I saw him.'

'No, you saw someone. Like your villagers making a monster out of a tramp. You only assumed it was Rory because you two are at odds again. You said the corridor was dim.'

'Yes, but …'

'Did it smell like Rory?'

I blinked at her baffled.

'Come on you must know what Rory smells like if you've been close. I could find my Merrit in a crowded room by smell alone.'

'I fear my olfactory senses are not as advanced as yours,' I said with as much dignity as I could muster in answering such a ridiculous question. But as I said it I remembered the sharp smell of the pine soap he favoured as I rested my head against his shoulder.

'There! There!' said Merry. 'That memory. Did you smell that?'

'No,' I said slowly, 'but I was busy trying to cower behind a pot of skinny leaves.'

Merry gave me a look that said she considered me a most unsatisfying companion in gossip and announced her intention of going back to sleep, as she had to get up early to start the range now that she was no longer allowed above stairs.

I was only too happy to let the conversation drop. It wasn't long before I heard her snores begin. I lay awake wracked with several disturbing trains of thought. I heard Merry murmur in her sleep: 'That many trees aren't natural.' There was something so normal and Merry-ish about her well-known dislike of the country that I found it comforting. I turned on my side and finally managed to slip into sleep.

The next morning I drank my cup of early morning tea in a fretful state. Should I tell Bertram what I had discovered or was it no-one's business but Rory's? If only I knew what was at stake here. Bertram wasn't Rory's employer, but I had no doubt he would tell Richard of his butler's misadventures. Bertram would be horrified. Richard

Stapleford would be amused. But either way Rory's reputation would be ruined. Did I have a right to do that? Maybe nothing had happened? Maybe she had simply lured him to her room on some pretence and he had made his excuses and left? Why was I so eager to condemn the man I had once loved. Perhaps because I …

'Have you heard a word I've said?' Susan was standing, hands on hips, in front of me. I knew this was not a happy stance. 'I'm sorry,' I said contritely. 'I didn't sleep well last night.'

'Seems like you're not the only one. Mr McLeod has just been telling me that Miss Flowers is yet to make an appearance at the breakfast table.'

Breakfast being of the normal buffet kind, my presence was not required in the morning room for this repast. 'Oh dear,' I said blankly, wondering what on earth this had to do with me.

'Well, I have orders to take the 'lady'[8] breakfast in her bedroom.'

'But she is neither ill nor married!' I exclaimed, these being the only two possible reasons for providing a lady with breakfast in bed. Indeed, I believe the thought of having breakfast in bed was urging Richenda to make her wedding plans come to fruition at a barely decent interval since her fiancé's mother's demise.

'I know,' said Susan. 'And I'm damn well not taking it up. You'll have to do it.'

'I can't!' I stammered.

'Well, you will bloody well have to!' snapped Susan, 'She'll have a fit if I send Merry up and I damn well can't send Mr McLeod into her bedroom!'

---

[8]The amount of vitriol Susan encompassed in this one word was masterly.

I wished for the ground to open up and swallow me.

As ever, my dearest wishes remained unanswered and a few short minutes later I was climbing the servants' stairs, this time, to Miss Flowers's bedroom. Susan had told me which room and I was fairly sure, despite my confused state and the dim lighting, it was the one I had seen Rory come out of. Once outside the door, I noticed a few tell-tale clods of mud from the plant pot. I'd have to come back up later and clear them up before anyone saw.

I balanced the tray on one hand and knocked. There was no answer. I knocked again a little louder. Still no answer. I considered putting the tray down in the corridor and making a bolt for it. But then I began feeling that something was wrong. I cannot say why. But in that moment I remembered the mystic, Madam Arcana, saying I had seen so many deaths that the dead were attracted to me. It was an unfortunate memory to recollect at that time. The hair on the back of my neck stood up and icy fingers played along my spine.

'Miss Flowers,' I said loudly, 'breakfast!' I realised I sounded rather like someone calling a dog in for dinner, but I would have been only too pleased if she opened the door to berate me.

She didn't.

I set the tray down on the floor in the hallway. I was thinking that if a sight – I couldn't even form the words in my mind to summon my suspicions to the forefront of my consciousness – it would be better not to have a lot of breakables in my hands.

I tried the door handle. The door was not locked. I opened it and went in. The curtains were still drawn and the room was in darkness. But I knew without a shadow of a doubt that no other living soul occupied that room. I rushed for the curtains, knocking a small chair out of my way in my hurry. I threw back the curtains and unexpected Scotch sunlight streamed in across the room. The bed was empty. More than empty – it had not been slept in. I was alone in the room.

Chapter Twelve:

The hunt

Bearing in mind my dual role, I quickly checked the wardrobe and dressing table drawers. They were full of female apparel, so whatever was happening, the woman hadn't absconded with secret papers or the like.

I took the breakfast tray back down with me on the grounds I'd have to fetch it at some point anyway.

'My food not good enough?' growled Jock when I re-entered the kitchen.

'She wasn't there,' I said.

'What?' asked Susan.

'No sign of her,' I sighed and added, because I knew Susan would discover this for herself, 'her bed's not been slept in.'

'The stupid wee lassie hasn't tried to do a bunk, has she?' said Jock. 'There's no transport up here for her to catch and she didnae look like the kind who'd have the sense to find her way through the countryside.'

'Or the shoes,' said the more practical Susan.

'Her clothes are still there,' I said.

'I'd better go and speak with Mr McLeod,' said Susan.

I sat down and Jock passed me a mug of tea. It seemed in the world of the Scots, as in the world of the English, all dilemmas are met with a medicinal intake of tea. For once, I drank the strong brew down gratefully. It might feel as if it was stripping the enamel from my teeth, but I needed fortifying. Merry who had been watching these exchanges silently suddenly piped up, 'Don't you think you should tell Susan about last night?'

See what I mean about Merry keeping secrets?

'I mean you should really have said something before she went and saw Rory,' said Merry trying to give a discreet signal and making such a hash of it that a vaudeville comedian couldn't have done better.

'Told me what?' said Susan, who had returned very quickly.

'I got up last night because I thought I heard a noise, but the doors and downstairs windows were all shut tight, so I assumed it was my imagination and didn't wake anyone.'

Susan sucked her teeth. 'It's true your last visit was a bit too eventful for anyone's liking, so it's not surprising that your imagination is playing tricks on you, but I'd be a might easier if you think you hear a noise if you wake me. I won't mind. Rather safe than sorry and I don't like to think of any young woman wandering this house alone at night. Not all threats come from outside, if you know what I mean,' she finished darkly.

'Miss Flowers?' I said, changing the subject quickly.

'Apparently, she has a habit of going swimming in the early morning.'

'But it would be freezing!' said Merry.

Susan shrugged. 'Yon sir man says she does it in all weathers. She thinks it helps keep her healthy.'

'I imagine it's more of a quick dip to tighten the skin,' I said, 'Richenda was keen to try it at the spa she's gone to.'

'I'm surprised it doesn't polish her off,' said Merry. 'Just thinking of it turns my bones cold.'

'But where would she go?' I asked.

'If she asked one of the locals and they took her at all seriously,' said Susan, 'they'd tell her about the big river about twenty minutes' hike from here. Of course, if she said she was a good swimmer they'd point her at the loch.'

'So I'll be meant to make the lassie a fresh feast whenever it suits herself to return,' said Jock, growling once more.

'Oh, I shouldn't think she'll be very long. She can have the leftovers from upstairs.'

'Oh aye,' said Jock, slightly mollified. 'I'll can put a wee bit by in the oven, I suppose.'

We all got on with our morning's work. I remembered to clear up the earth upstairs. I thought no more about Miss Flowers until I finally returned to the kitchen for the servants' early meal before we served luncheon. There was a smell of burning and Jock was scraping the remains of breakfast into a bucket. 'She didn't want breakfast?' I asked.

'She's no come back,' said Jock darkly.

Rory strode into the kitchen. 'Everyone,' he said in a commanding tone, 'we are to get up a search for Miss Flowers.'

'And will they be wanting their luncheon while we are to be out searching?' said Susan. 'Or do they think the ghosties will be serving it to them?'

'At this stage, Mrs Simpson, the search will involve Mr Bertram Stapleford, myself, and any of the local men on the estate who can be spared.'

'That's the way it should be,' piped up Jock, articulating far too clearly for once. 'It's no right to ask a young woman to go looking for a body.'

'No one has said anything about bodies,' said Rory sharply.

'So you'll be hunting ghosties then?' said Jock

belligerently. 'A body, Mr McLeod, is a body whether it be deid or alive, and if yon lassie has been missing in the countryside for hours on end, it's unlikely she's come to a guid end.'

'I'm sure she was no better than she ought to be,' said Susan obscurely, 'but none of us want the silly minx to come to harm.'

'I'll be reminding you, Mrs Simpson, that you are talking about one of those upstairs,' said Rory stiffly.

I gave him my most withering glance. He turned on me at once. 'Is there something you wish to add, Euphemia?'

'Not at all, Mr McLeod. I'm sure you have matters well in hand.' I hoped the irony glittered from my eyes, but Rory brushed me aside.

'You can manage luncheon without me. Merry can serve again upstairs for now.'

Merry mouthed, 'Oh I can, can I?' behind Rory's back, but when he turned round she nodded demurely. Rory scowled again. 'And no interfering, Euphemia,' he said and stormed out.

'As if I would want anything to do with Miss Flowers,' I said crossly, but admittedly when he was out of earshot.

'Do you think anything has happened to her?' asked Merry with a frown of concern.

'I was thinking, Susan, seeing how it's the men that have missed her they might …'

'Not of thought of searching the house,' finished Susan for me. 'Daft bint might well have got herself shut in somewhere.'

'There certainly aren't any local folk round here that would do her harm,' said Jock challengingly. 'No matter what the nobs might say. We're a civilised lot up here.' Then he returned, abruptly, to clattering among his pans and talking incomprehensibly once more.

'I'll get the bootboy to search the house,' said Susan. 'If there's one person in this lodge that knows all its nooks and crannies it's that wee man. The times I've hunted high and low for him to come and do his chores and not found hide nor hair of him!'

I nodded. 'Right, Merry! Fresh aprons! We'll be serving luncheon in a trice. Are they having soup again, Jock?'

'Aye.'

Merry groaned.

In the event we could both have been serving live crabs in our corsets and the gentlemen of the house would have taken no notice of us. They whispered among themselves in low tight voices, and the senior man at the head of the table barely lifted his eyes from his plate, except when one of the whispers became too loud for him, when he gave whoever had spoken a ferocious stare.

Back in the kitchen Merry asked, 'Is it just me or are that lot a might bit upset over some strumpet of a secretary? Not that I'm saying her life is worth less than anyone else's, but you know what that lot are like.' She inclined her head towards the upstairs.

'They do seem to be taking her disappearance to heart,' I said.

'What exactly are they meeting about?' asked Merry.

'I have no idea.'

'Euphemia, you always have an idea. Out with it.'

'No, this time, honestly, Merry, I don't have a clue what is going on.'

'Hmmm,' said Merry, 'then I'm betting we're in for a whole mess of trouble.'

The day wore on. The boot boy reported that despite

assiduously searching the Lodge there was no sign of the lady. Rory and Bertram stumbled into the kitchen shortly before it was time to dine. Both of them were muddy, and their faces lined with fatigue. Bertram sat down on a kitchen stool and began to undo his boots. 'I reckon I've tramped over half of bloody Scotland,' he said.

'Mr Stapleford!' said Susan, hovering nervously by the kitchen table.

'What?' said Bertram blankly.

'This is a place we prepare food, Mr Stapleford,' I said with a slight smile. 'Not really somewhere muddy boots and sweaty tweeds are welcome.'

'My tweeds are not sweaty,' protested Bertram. Then he blushed red. 'That didn't come out quite as I meant it,' he said.

'There is a boot room, if you recall, sir,' said Rory with dignity.

'Oh, yes,' said Bertram as if he had been reminded of a treasure trove. 'Excellent idea. Merry, could you pop upstairs and run me a quick bath before dinner.'

'It will be my pleasure to do that for you, sir,' said Rory quickly.

I sniffed a bit too loudly

'Yes, Euphemia?'

'Oh nothing, Mr McLeod, it's a fine thing to see you concerned over the reputations of your female staff.'

Rory's mouth opened, but it was Bertram's voice that came out. 'Oh for heaven's sake, will you two stop sniping at each other! I'm not asking you to kiss and make up,' continued Bertram, 'but I for one am sick of the atmosphere you bring into every room you are in together.'

'I am sorry if I am not providing satisfaction,' said Rory stiffly. 'Would you care for my resignation?'

Bertram stood up in his stockinged feet with his boots in one hand. 'Oh don't be a blithering idiot, man!' he said, and thrust the boots at Rory. 'Mrs Simpson, I hope you've been working your staff hard. I could eat a horse tonight. Including the shoes. Your countryside certainly works up an appetite for a man.' And with that he stalked out with as much dignity as a man in his socks can muster.[9]

Of course, both Rory and I were embarrassed, but after the various situations the three of us had found ourselves in together we did not function as normal master and servants. We both eyed each other askance. Rory gave me a slight nod which I returned. It was a taciturn agreement not to spat again in public, but certainly there was no sign of an olive branch from either of us.

After our silent exchange I became aware that we had an audience. Merry, Susan and Jock were standing with expressions of disbelief on their faces. 'Cor blimey,' said Merry, 'if I behaved like you two I'd been out on my ear before I had time to draw breath.'

'There was me thinking they must do things differently down south,' added Jock.

Susan's mouth opened and closed, but no sound came out.

Rory drew himself up to his full height, and despite the flush in his cheeks attempted to reassert his authority. 'Let us not forget that there is a young lady missing.'

I still sniffed, but I did it much more softly. Rory marched out, holding Bertram's boots aloft as if they were plated in silver, not covered in the smelliest Scotch mud.

'He's right, you know,' chimed in Merry. 'I reckon if she's not been found by now then something bad will have

---

[9]Which, given his socks were red and orange, was not very much.

happened to her.'

'Mah meat's beginning to singe,' said Jock, bringing our attention back to the matter in hand. No matter what was happening outside our small world, dinner must still be served.

Chapter Thirteen:

The police come and go – and are not liked very much

It was a house at odds that went to bed that night. One of the men had decided the police should be called. Given the secrecy of this meeting, I had half expected the mysterious Mr Edward, the largely British-based counterpart to Fitzroy to turn up, but the only man summoned was the local bobby. He arrived on a wobbly bicycle very late after dinner.

The constable who appeared could not have been more than nineteen. He had unfortunate carrotty red hair, an extremely freckled complexion, and buck teeth. He did not inspire confidence. First of all he spoke to 'them upstairs' as he was later to refer to Bertram and his guests. By the way he descended on the kitchen, he had formed the strong impression from whatever had been said to him that those below stairs were responsible for the missing Miss Flowers.

He gathered Merry, Rory, Jock, Susan, and me in the kitchen. The bootboy with remarkable sense had retreated to one of his secret hiding places.

'All I am saying is that it will go easier on yous if you 'fess up now.' The constable planted his feet wide apart, held his notebook open, licked his pencil, and waited confidently for one of us to confess.

I could practically feel Rory beside me straightening his spine and looking down in astonishment at this creature before him.

Merry, candid as ever, said, 'You've got to be bleedin' kidding! None of us have done nuffink!'

Susan put her hands on her hips and said, 'If you don't start behaving with a bit more respect I'll be having words with your mother, young Derek McClintock.' Then she added her master stroke. 'Why, I remember you when you were only a wee bairn in smelly nappies. Come to think of it, I probably changed a few for your Ma.' She gave him a look that suggested she remembered those days all too well.

But 'wee' McClintock was made of stern stuff. He licked his pencil again and flicked through his notebook. 'From what I've been informed by them upstairs, you,' he jabbed his pencil suddenly at Merry, 'the lady in question had demanded your dismissal after your abysmal service.'

'It were an accident,' exclaimed Merry hotly. 'And who the 'ell said I was abysmal!'

But young Derek had not finished. 'You are her best friend,' he said turning his pointy pencil at me next, and gesturing at Merry. 'Thick as thieves by all accounts. Always have each other's backs.'

'This is preposterous,' began Rory.

'Now, I'm not saying it might not have started out as a prank. I understand the lady in question was young, pretty, and doing extremely well for herself despite her lower-class beginnings. It would be easy to see how someone who'd had a much harder life ... you, for instance, Mrs Simpson!' And he swung his pencil at Susan.

Jock growled loudly. 'If you're thinking of swinging your wee pencil in my direction, laddie, think again. I've a fine collection of knives in this kitchen and I keep them

91

sharp.'

Derek scribbled frantically in his notebook. He wrote with his tongue hanging out, carefully enunciating each word. 'A declaration of a violent tendency!' Jock gave what can only be described as a roar and reached for his cleaver.

Rory stepped smoothly in the way. 'As I understand it no evidence of foul play has been discovered. I am of course not privy to what our masters upstairs may have condescended to tell you, but I assure you that you are verging on defamation of character. Unless you have some grounds for the persecution you are inflicting on us I suggest you get back on your bicycle, go home, and think how you will conduct the search for the doubtless still alive Miss Flowers.' And with this he swung open the kitchen door. 'Out,' he said.

Jock growled and raised his cleaver. 'I will be back,' said Constable McClintock.

Jock took a step forward and young Derek fled into the darkness.

Merry thumbed her nose at him. 'Good riddance to bad rubbish,' she called after him.

'Well, didn't he grow up to be a wee bugger?' said Susan in a rare moment of candour.

'I fear we have not seen the last of him, Mrs Simpson,' said Rory. 'I also fear that we will have to talk to him.'

'You think she's dead,' said Merry flatly.

'As I understand it Miss Flowers took no clothing or monies with her, so we are left with the options that she decided to walk home to London, has been kidnapped, has simply vanished like Highland mist, or that something unfortunate has occurred.'

'She could have had an accident,' said Merry – perhaps a little too hopefully.

'Indeed,' said Rory, 'I was not for one moment suggesting – bar the faint possibility of a kidnapping – that anything nefarious had happened to the young lady.'

'Do they teach all 'em big words in butlering school?' said Merry. 'Make you study your books into the night.'

Rory scowled, 'As you well know, Mary, there is no such thing as a butlering school! Now, I suggest we all get some sleep, so we can be ready for whatever tomorrow will bring.'

'It's Merry,' muttered Merry.

Rory was on his way out, but we heard him say quite distinctly, 'Not according to Mrs Lewis.'

I for one was more than happy to get into bed. I had found the day emotionally and physically exhausting. I had already began to long to see Richenda again and found myself thinking of her with some affection, which surprised me. As her companion, I no longer had to sweep, clean, and serve – the Lodge had given me a harsh lesson in the realities of a maid's life as opposed to the more comfortable life as a Lady's Companion. I would never again complain of being bored. I would take up hobbies, I vowed. Anything was better than washing stairs. How my back ached. How did Merry manage this day in and day out? How had I managed it? I felt truly bone weary as I climbed into bed ready for nothing more than a deep and dreamless sleep. Merry, however, did not have the same idea.

'Do you think she's been murdered?' she asked, sitting up in bed and all too wide awake.

'Why on earth would anyone wish to harm her?'

'It could be a wandering lunatic,' said Merry. 'Or maybe a jealous lover? Or maybe …'

'Merry, have you been reading periodicals?' I

shuddered, barely able to say the next words, 'or dramatic novels?'

Merry ignored my questions, confirming to my mind my suspicions. 'You're ever so good at finding dead bodies. Maybe we should send you out and let you wander around a bit. You're better than a dog chasing rabbits. I'm sure you'd scare up a dead body or two.'

'Or two!' I exclaimed. 'Honestly, Merry, stop with this ridiculousness. You'll give us both nightmares.'

'But you do think something's bad happened, don't you?' persisted Merry.

'I can't say I anticipate a happy outcome,' I confessed.[10]

'So you do think she's been murdered!'

'No, I think this foolishness of using cold water to tighten the skin has been the end of her. It might be all very well to do it on some spa somewhere, but I doubt she anticipated the freezing cold of Scotch water.'

'You think she's been killed by the cold?' said Merry in a voice of disbelief. 'How very dull.'

'But still very final,' I said. 'And now, Merry, I am going to sleep.' I lay down, turned on my side and pulled the covers over my head.

I was midway through a dream in which I was explaining to Rory the correct way to eat lobster. I should note here I have no idea how to eat lobster. We were sitting by the side of a beautiful lake, or maybe loch; the dream hadn't revealed the specifics yet. The day was glorious and Rory, I felt sure, was about to offer me an engagement ring made from stardust and sunshine, when the loch or lake made an alarming loud belch and gave up

---

[10]The importance of being truthful, learned at my father's knee, has caused me much difficulty throughout my life.

its dead. The body of the late Miss Flowers floated over to us. Her face was ringed with aspidistra leaves, her eyes wide and dark with death. She parted blue lips and said, 'For God's sake, Euphemia, wake up!'

I shot up in bed. My heart was clamouring in my chest as if it wished nothing more than to escape its place. My skin was slick with perspiration. I could feel myself shaking. In the darkness I could just make out Merry's sleeping form.

'Euphemia!'

I gave a little shriek and pinched myself.

'For God's sake, Euphemia, wake up. Before I set the whole bloody household on us.' The exasperation in Bertram's tone more than anything brought me back to reality. I got up and struggled into my dressing gown in the dark. I tied back my hair roughly.

'I'm coming,,' I whispered as aloud as I dared. 'I need to make myself decent.'

He stopped banging on the door at that, but I could practically hear his impatience. Merry, always a deep sleeper, missed the very excitement she had been pining for. Finally I opened the door. I was relieved to see he was fully dressed and apparently sober. Although in this regard I had learned that appearances of sobriety in gentlemen can be most misleading.

'What on earth is it, Bertram, that you must come to my bedchamber in such an inappropriate manner?'

'It's Rory,' said Bertram. 'I rather fear he's murdered Miss Flowers.'

Chapter Fourteen:

A difficult night with difficult people

My first reaction was one of disbelief. 'No!' I said firmly.

'I'm afraid so, Euphemia. There is little other explanation.'

'No, no and no,' I said emphatically. 'Not only is Rory no murderer, but for him to be accused again in his homeland is ludicrous!' [11] 'It is without the bounds of possibility,' I added for emphasis, and to show that Rory wasn't the only one who had an extensive vocabulary. [12] I reached out and gave Bertram a pinch on the arm.

'Oi!' he said in a most ungentlemanly and rather alarmed way.

'Just checking I was awake.'

'Aren't you meant to pinch yourself,' he said petulantly, rubbing his arm.

'I've done that but you could still be a hallucination. What you're saying is preposterous.'

'Look, I know you're still damn well in love with the fellow ...'

---

[11] I refer here to a previous adventure. Well, it wasn't so much an adventure as a nightmare, but Merry called it an adventure.

[12] Yes, I know Bertram wasn't around for that particular conversation, but in my defence I was still only half-present in the waking world.

'Mr Stapleford!' I said in the outraged tone of a Duchess.

'Oh, for God's sake, just come with me. He's in the library.'

'Have you called the police?' I asked.

'Not yet.'

'All right,' I conceded. 'I will come with you despite the hour, if only to save you from your own foolishness.'

Bertram muttered something under his breath about God saving him from difficult females. I decided to feign deafness. It was inconceivable that Merry would not soon awaken if we continued our discussion here and the last thing I wanted was Merry weaving stories about tonight's doings. Bertram isn't a naturally imaginative man, but he is a passionate one, and once convinced he is in the right he is staunch in his stance. Or, some might say, as stubborn-headed as a mule.

I followed him through the house to the library. The rest of the rooms appeared to be shut up and dark. Good, no one else was in on this.

'Who did you leave guarding Rory? Jock?' I asked.

'No one,' said Bertram. 'He gave me his word he would await our return.'

'Bertram, you do realise if he was a murderer that would have been a very stupid thing to have done.'

'A gentleman's word, Euphemia!'

'The word of a man you suggest is a killer. The last time I checked, murderers weren't generally described as honourable.'

Bertram did not answer, but quickened his pace enough that by the time we arrived at the library I was more than a little breathless. He threw open the library door and stormed in as if was preparing to wrestle Rory to the ground mid-escape attempt. I followed more slowly behind, but I was in time to witness the expression on Rory's face. He had been warming himself by the embers of the fire. He turned towards us and sneered at Bertram. This response made me feel my first qualm. Rory, the butler, would never display his displeasure with those he considered his superiors, even when he witnessed the often extremely poor behaviour of the so called upper classes.

'Did you think I would go back on my word?' Rory said coldly. 'I may not be a gentleman, but my word is my bond.'

'I didn't,' said Bertram flushing, 'but Euphemia ...'

Rory turned to me, his face furious. I held up my hand. 'No, don't drag me in to this display of male bravado! I merely said that no murderer could be trusted to keep their word,' Rory started to speak, but I spoke over him, 'BUT,' I shouted, 'I said there was no way I would ever believe you could be a murderer.'

Rory deflated before my eyes. 'I'm sorry, Euphemia.'

'I will always believe in you,' I said.

Rory moved towards me, his hands outstretched. A look from Bertram checked him.

'I am afraid I still have the most serious doubts,' Bertram said. 'I require an explanation that gives a good reason for your actions.'

Rory's face closed in upon itself and he stepped back again. 'I have already said I have nothing to say to you, Bertram Stapleford.' Hostility was written in every line of Rory's body. The two men stood opposite one another, glowering.

'If you do not provide an explanation I will be forced to hand you over to the police, McLeod.'

'So I understand,' said Rory, coldly.

'Oh for heaven's sake.' I almost said 'boys'. 'The two of you are behaving like children. Will one of you kindly tell me what is going on?'

Bertram said, 'Very well. I found Rory searching Miss Flowers's room. Doubtless removing evidence.'

'What were you doing in her room?'

'Exactly my question!' said Bertram.

'No, I meant you, Bertram?' Rory's lips twitched at this.

'I heard a noise,' said Bertram with extreme dignity.

'But why were you prowling around at night?' I asked.

'I do not prowl,' growled Bertram, momentarily looking for all the world like a badly bearded tiger. 'Anyway, I am not the one on trial here.'

'So it's trial I'm on, is it?' said Rory, becoming alarmingly Scotch. 'And you'll be judge, jury, and executioner, man, will you?'

'I didn't mean that,' blustered Bertram.

'Enough,' I said, my patience snapping. 'I am not a butler able to swan around the place. Nor am I guest of the house. I am a maid. A maid! As a maid I scrub stairs, beat carpets, make beds, and generally spend the entire day working until when it finally comes to my overly late bed time – when I get to have a few short hours well-deserved sleep – I am tired. I am sore. And after an extremely long and tiring day I am awoken during my very few hours of allotted and well-earned sleep, dragged from my bed, and brought here to listen to the two of you bicker about ridiculous accusations. I am not a happy lady. Do you both understand that?'

Neither of them actually said 'Yes, Euphemia,' but they both looked suitably sheepish.

'Now, both of you, sit down!' I can at times summon my mother's demeanour and this proved to be one of them. Both men exchanged glances united for a moment in the male fear of what they all too often deem mysterious female behaviour. Under my steely gaze they sat. At this point I realised I had never been quite so angry with either of them.

'Bertram, why were you up so late?'

'I was trying to discover what our guests were involved in,' said Bertram. 'It's damn difficult trying to do whatever Fitzroy wants us to do when we don't know what it is.'

I couldn't but help agree with that. 'Why do you assume that Rory was not doing the same?'

'He's a butler,' said Bertram.

'Meaning I'm not important enough to think for myself?' asked Rory indignantly.

'Quiet, Rory, you'll get your chance.' I spoke dismissively, as if talking to an errant child. Few men are proof against this tone when they deserve it and he lapsed into silence.

'More precisely, Bertram why did you think Rory was up to no good? Did you also know about his affair with Miss Flowers?'

Both men spoke simultaneously and loudly. 'I cannot hear you if you both talk at once,' I said, but I had pushed it too far.

'I understand you're tired, Euphemia,' said Rory, 'but no man can take being talked down to by a woman like this.'

Bertram made a muttering noise which was probably an agreement.

Rory continued, 'I have no idea why you think I was having an affair with Miss Flowers. It may be common practice in whatever houses you have visited for there to be upstairs-downstairs trysts, but I have my standards. I would never condone such practice in a member of my staff, let alone indulge in it myself. And as for a woman like Miss Flowers!'

'Exactly,' said Bertram, seeming to forget he and Rory had ever been at odds. 'No man in his right mind would have a dalliance with her.' I expected him to make some comment about her vulgarity, but he surprised me by saying, 'Far too scheming by half. That woman's a shark if ever I've seen one.'

'Agreed,' said Rory tersely.

'But what were you doing in her room last night?' I asked.

'I have never been in her room afore tonight,' said Rory.

'But I saw you!' I protested.

'So now who's been prowling?' said Bertram. Rory and I ignored him. 'I give you my word,' said Rory, meeting my eye.

I closed my eyes and ran through the scene again in my mind's eye. 'Oh, the aspidistra,' I said.

'Is this some kind of code word?' asked Bertram, 'Because Fitzroy didn't mention ...'

'I must have got turned around when I was wrestling with it.' I thought hard. 'That means I saw you come out of the library.'

'Aye, I was there,' said Rory.

'Why?' demanded Bertram. 'And what were you doing, Euphemia?'

'I was woken by a noise. I couldn't work out what it was, but I tracked it down to this corridor. It's amazing how sound carries through a silent house at night. It was Miss Flowers laughing – well, giggling.'

'And you saw me coming out of what you thought was her room. Och, Euphemia, I hoped you thought better of me than that.'

I felt myself go red. 'Sorry,' I said very quietly.

'We seem to have explained everything now except

Rory's repeated nocturnal ramblings,' declared Bertram.

'I have no intention of explaining myself. I resign.'

'Well, leaving aside it's not me you work for,' said Bertram acidly, 'I cannot in good conscience let you leave this house before the woman in question is found.'

'And how exactly do you plan to stop me?' said Rory rising from his seat. He had at least three inches on Bertram in height and was half again as wide at the shoulders.

'Don't you dare threaten Bertram,' I snapped. 'You know he has a weak heart.'

'Euphemia, I do not need you to defend me,' cried Bertram, but he was looking a little pale around the gills Rory glanced at his face and must have seen this too as he sat down again.

'Why did you have to bring her into it?' he said plaintively to Bertram.

'I thought you might tell her the truth. I'm more than aware you hold Euphemia in high esteem and that you think little of me.'

Rory winced. 'You're one of the better toffs I've met,' he said.

'Rory, we are at an impasse until you tell us what you were doing. Please,' I begged, 'I really do want to get back to my bed.'

'Och, very well, if you must have it. I was looking for maps.'

Chapter Fifteen:

In which things are both more and less than they seem

This time it was Bertram who pinched himself. 'Maps?' he said in incredulous tones. His face wore an expression that suggested should Rory have declared his intention to fly to the moon he would have found it more believable.

'Oh good grief,' I said. I had the awful feeling that a great deal more conversation would be needed before this situation was resolved. I thought wistfully of my bed. 'Why,' I said as calmly and reasonably as I could, 'were you looking for maps, Rory. Did you want to go for a walk?'

Both men levelled a cold hard stare in my direction, but really I could think of no other reason for wanting a map.

'Ask him,' said Rory, he jerked his head towards Bertram. 'He's English!'

'So am I, but I have no idea what you're talking about.'

'Of course not,' said Rory, 'you're a female.'

'If either of you dare to say this is beyond my little brain I shall do something drastic with that poker!'

Bertram slumped back into his chair. 'Well, it's certainly beyond my little brain.'

'You're telling me you've no idea what the Westminster government is planning to do with my country?'

'Rory, do I strike you as a political figure? I'm never going to be a man of the state. Why, I can't even keep my roof on my own home.'[13]

Rory stopped scowling. 'I suppose it would be more believable if your brother was in involved in this.'

'And you know how likely I am to do him a favour,' said Bertram.

'Aye, all right,' said Rory. 'Maybe ye dinnae ken, but you'll no be one to be stopping it.'

'What? For heaven's sake, what?' My voice verged on the edge of a scream.

'They're only going to go and cut Scotland off from the rest of Great Britain. Annex it like some forgotten county. No doubt leaving us all up here to rot.'

'That's ludicrous,' said Bertram. 'What are they going to do? Build a wall?'

'Aye,' said Rory, still sounding ridiculously Scotch as he does when he is very upset. 'Only the Highlands, mind. They're keeping the rich southern areas that are fine for farming. The rest is cast off.'

'Good God, man!' exclaimed Bertram. 'No man in his right mind would do that. Where would one go for the shooting? Where would we get pheasant to eat?'

'Nice to hear you appreciate my country for something,' said Rory sarcastically.

I attempted to be the voice of reason once more. 'Rory, you've obviously seen something. Can you show us?'

'I didnae take the maps. That would have aroused suspicions.'

'But you are sure you saw them,' I persisted. 'Some

---

[13]This was a reference to Bertram's hugely mistaken purchase of his home in the fens, White Orchards, which had begun to fall down as soon as it was put up.

dreams can have the semblance of reality.'

Rory addressed Bertram, 'When you left me in here you said you were off to find someone to shed reason on tonight and you got her?'

'I thought you might be more likely to talk to her. And you have been.'

'Were you searching Miss Flowers's room for the maps?'

'Aye, I thought with her missing I wouldnae be disturbed. And she was secretary like so I thought it was a good chance she kept watch over the papers.'

'And you assumed he was going to remove evidence rather than search for proof.'

Bertram nodded.

'Well, it all seems very simple to me. We must all go and search Miss Flowers's room.'

'But the police ...' protested Bertram.

'Exactly. They will be back tomorrow. And if you take a look through that window you'll see we are fast heading towards dawn. We must act quickly.'

There was some more ranting about who believed whom and who had been unreasonably suspicious of whom. Bertram also went off a fair bit about messing with police procedure. I left them to it, crossed the hall and quietly opened Miss Flowers's bedroom door. I went over to the window and drew back one of the drapes. The blue-grey light of the early morning flooded the room. Traces of the night's darkness lingered and the light did not seem to fully reach the corners of the room. The scene had a strange, dream-like quality. The natural colours were all changed in a way that made the room look as if it was underwater.

There's a feeling rooms have when someone is gone. I've noticed it before when I have entered into the room of a deceased person. You might say it is my imagination, but to see all their things laid out as they were last used, used by an owner who had no doubt he or she would be using them again, left lying forlorn, does something to my insides. I picked up Miss Flowers's hairbrush. A cheap sort with harsh bristles and a wooden back, strands of her hair still clung to it. Absent-mindedly I picked them out and put them in the waste paper bin in much the same way as she might have done. I sat down and looked into her dressing table mirror. No shade looked back at me. I saw no reflection but my own. I was simply intently aware of her absence. I knew she was dead.

On the dressing table was set out a cheap but gaudy collection of facial cosmetics. I felt a twinge of sympathy for the woman that had nothing to do with whatever her fate had been. I had judged her unkindly. As someone else had said, she had been a poor girl trying to make good. And look where it had got her! Secretary to someone in the government. Not, I thought, a proper civil service type of job, but note-taking, tea-making, and being useful. Being so useful, in fact, that she was brought to a secret meeting in the Highlands when such pains had been taken to keep the rest of the world at bay. Had it all been too tempting? Had she somehow taken advantage of the situation? Taken advantage, but been caught?

I knew how ruthless Fitzroy could be. He did not hesitate to kill if he felt it was in the interests of his King and country. Could someone here be like him? But, none of the men I had encountered had struck me as having the cold compassionless steel within them that Fitzroy could display. If I hadn't known better I would have thought the four Smiths were no more than businessmen. Not in any way connected to the government. Almost like superior tradesmen. Could Rory be right? Could they actually be building a wall? Bertram's protests, were of course, ridiculous, but I couldn't think of a single reason for such a huge undertaking unless there had been some epidemic of illness in the Highlands and the government sought to protect the rest of the population. My heart thudded harder at this as I thought of the strange creature I had fled from in the forest. Could there be some kind of Highland plague?

I felt panic about to engulf me. Could a government do such a cruel thing to its people? Condemn some to die so the rest might live? Fitzroy would say it was necessary not cruel. A bead of perspiration trickled along my hairline and down onto my forehead. Was I already ill? I half-rose, ready to bolt back to the study, to safety – but none of us would be safe …

The cold reason of sanity cut through my morbid imaginings. I could almost hear Rory shooting down my suspicions with 'Do you really think such a meeting would be arranged within the infectious area?' No, of course, it wouldn't be. I sat back down and began going methodically through the dressing table drawers. My heart still beat too fast. I felt tired, edgy, and longed for nothing more than to see Richenda's long horsy face and hear her demanding more cake.

There was nothing in the dressing table that I did not expect to find. The men still had not joined me, but at least they had had the sense to lower their voices. I could no longer hear their bickering and that was some relief.

I went next for her wardrobe. I searched both the clothes, including pockets and went through her suitcase. I tempered my urge to get out of the room with an attempt not to overly disturb things. Nothing.

As is always the way just as I was about to give up I found them. Under the mattress. Of course, the natural

108

hiding place of all those with few resources. A small flat satchel. The catch opened easily, unlocked. Within I could see neatly folded squares of paper. This had to be it. I took one last look around the room. It did not look to me as if it had been disturbed. Perhaps an expert like Fitzroy would have known, but our local constable was as close to his league as a dung beetle was to a phoenix. I closed the drapes, and taking the satchel with me in its entirety, closed the door on Miss Flowers bedroom. I heartily hoped I would never have to enter the room again. I would find some favour I could exchange with Merry, so she would be the one to clear it when the police allowed.

I returned to library to find Bertram and Rory on their feet, fists up, facing off at one other. Behind them the sun rose in the sky, flooding light across the room and sending their shadows tapering long and thin against the walled shelves.

'I have it,' I said. They both turned to look at me. As one their eyes locked on the satchel I held up. 'But it is daybreak. We will have to discuss this later.'

Then I turned on my heel, the satchel under my arm, and headed as fast as common sense allowed for my bed. I might yet gain a full thirty minutes of sleep before my duties summoned me. As I hurried away, I sensed the frustration of the men left behind. After all the trouble they had caused me they could wait a few hours to sort out this nonsense. Of course there would be no wall.

Chapter Sixteen:

In which Bertram shows an unforeseen talent

We managed to gather shortly after breakfast in Rory's parlour when the meeting upstairs began again in earnest. Merry had followed me intrigued. I was counting on Rory to send her on her way. I thought my discouraging her would only make her more inquisitive. Her eyes widened when she saw Bertram sitting with his feet up on Rory's side table. Rory, fastidious as ever, did not look too happy, but said nothing. At least Bertram had not yet brought out his pipe.

To my surprise neither man bade Merry leave. Rory reported there had been a hushed and urgent conversation over breakfast on whether the police should again be contacted. 'Yon ministry man made it clear he felt they had wasted enough time. He said they had been informed and it was not their duty to do more.'

'Mr Bald was right grumpy about that,' said Merry who had served morning tea.

'Mr Who?' said Rory.

'I can't go on calling them all Mr Smith, can I?'

'To their faces, I sincerely hope you can,' said Rory.

'Obviously,' said Merry.

'What do you call them?' asked Bertram. I could see his curiosity was torn between seeing the satchel (which I had hidden in easy reach, but neither of the two men had found) and delving into the remarkable inner world of Merry.

'Mr Bald, Mr Beard, Mr Nose, and Mr Short.'

They were all instantly recognisable. It had been Mr Short who had sent me with the letter. 'I reckon he fancied his chances with her,' said the plain-speaking Merry.

'Do you not have duties to attend to?' said Rory disapprovingly.

'What about Euphemia?' protested Merry.

'Euphemia is senior staff,' said Rory stiffly. 'We must discuss what has happened.'

'She's a maid, like me!'

'You know that isn't true, Merry,' said Bertram gently. 'It really would be better if you left.'

'You lot are up to something, aren't you?' cried Merry indignantly. I knew her well enough that she had no problem with us being up to something. Her problem was solely with not being included. 'I'll tell Susan if you don't let me …'

'Enough,' said Rory fiercely. 'You know me well enough, lassie, to know I would never respond to blackmail.'

'But you can't exclude me!' said Merry. 'I'm Stapleford Hall like the rest of you.'

'This time, Merry, we can and we will,' said Bertram gently but firmly ushering her out of the door. She might have pushed against Rory, but she would never do that with a Stapleford. She had been with the family since childhood. Bertram closed the door behind her. Shortly afterwards we heard the kitchen back door slam.

'Oh dear,' I said. 'I'm sorry I couldn't get rid of her without raising her suspicions. I thought if we were boring enough she might wander off, but you proved far too interesting, the both of you.'

'The maps, Euphemia,' said Rory through gritted teeth.

I reached behind him and pulled the satchel from behind a small bookcase. 'Good grief, do you mean,' he began, but I was already spreading the maps out on the small table. Rory was right. They were of the local Highlands and two strong lines were drawn across the breadth of the Scottish mainland. They diverged slightly, but completed much the same path.

'Two options?' I suggested.

'That's what I think,' said Rory, his face dark with anger.

Bertram drew up a chair and sat down. 'Good gracious me. I'd never have believed it.'

'I telt ye,' said Rory.

'It's impossible,' said Bertram. 'Quite impossible. That something like this could be considered is remarkable. What a feat of engineering.'

Rory gave a low growl. 'It's a Great fuckin' Wall, man, not some fuckin' automaton.'

'Rory!' I cried, horrified.

'How would you feel it they wanted to wall you in, Euphemia?'

'It isn't a wall,' said Bertram flatly.

'What do you mean, man?' demanded Rory. 'Yer can see the line for yerself.'

'Yes, I can,' said Bertram. 'In fact I've seen quite a lot of these markings in my time. You might be a sublime butler, Rory, but you have no idea how to read a map.'

'So what is that, then?' said Rory. He traced the line along the top map. 'This bollocking great line that splits my homeland in half.'

'That,' said Bertram, with complete confidence, 'is a canal.'

'A canal,' I echoed blankly. 'Are you sure?'

'The Fens are littered with canals and lifetimes of attempts at draining water away. If there's one thing I've learned to recognise on a map, now I live in that dratted swampland, it's a man-made waterway.'

The colour drained from Rory's face. He sunk into hard-backed chair by the table. 'But why would they do that?' He asked. 'Are they trying to turn Scotland in an island? That's worse than a wall.'

Bertram leaned forward over the map studying it. 'It's a wide canal,' he said, 'it's true, but see this here?' he pointed to a smudged marking. 'I think that's some kind of bridge. And that and that. That might even be a tunnel. None of those markings look quite how I think they should. No idea what the dotted lines mean.'

'Why would they want a canal through Scotland?' said Rory. 'I ken the English are all a wee bittie daft ...'

'Where does it start?' I asked. 'Does that tell us anything?'

Bertram peered closely. (He is slightly short-sighted.) 'Near the Clydebank area.' He paused. 'Oh, God,' he said. 'I was hoping this was some sort of stupid hoax, some political prank Fitzroy's people might be playing, but I can think why they might do this. Why some people might want it done.' He face filmed with sweat and he went white around the mouth.

'Quickly,' I said to Rory, 'loosen his collar! Bertram's about to have one of his turns.' I ran into the kitchen for water. Bertram had moved to the more comfortable wing-back by the fire. I wondered if Rory had lifted him. His collar was open and his tie askew. He took the glass from me with slightly shaking hands. 'It's all right, Euphemia. I'm not going to have a heart attack this time. It's just a shock realising what this must mean.'

'But what can it mean, man?' demanded Rory.

'It means we are on the eve of war,' said Bertram.

'With Scotland?' said Rory, alarmed.

'With Germany,' said Bertram. 'With the great German Empire.'

Chapter Seventeen:

In which we discover the end of the world will not come today, but that tomorrow is looking distinctly dodgy

'I don't understand,' said Rory. 'Are you sure you're feeling yourself, Mr Bertram?'

'What are they building on the Clyde, Rory?'

'Ships,' said Rory. 'Liners for around the world.'

'Not just civilian shipping,' said Bertram. 'Dreadnoughts.'

I had read enough of the newspapers during my recent incarceration in Stapleford Hall to recognise the name. 'The new breed of warship?' I asked.

'The biggest warships Britain – sorry, Rory, Scotland, has ever built,' said Bertram.

I picked up the edge of one of the maps. There, very faintly, ran a pencilled script. I read it aloud. 'The Kiel Canal. You're right, Bertram. It is a canal.'

'It's a short cut,' said Rory disbelieving. 'Rather than sail the ships round the top of Scotland, which I grant you is the roughest sea in the world. Ships are lost there all the time. But it looks like they're not even prepared to go round the southern edge of England. They'd rather cut the heart out of Scotland.'

'That's terrible. Why would they do that?'

'It's obvious,' said Bertram. I noted with concern his

breathing had yet to return to normal. 'It's because they think they won't have the time. They expect the Germans to mass their navy any day.'

'This will take more than a day to dig,' said Rory. 'And I tell you, the local people won't simply stand by.'

'They will claim that for the safety of us all, for the sake of King and country, it must be built so we can be ready when Germany declares war. It means they think war with Germany, be it one year or four years away, is inevitable.'

'But it's 1912,' I cried. 'Surely we are beyond such barbarity!'

'Dear God,' muttered Bertram into his glass, 'the things I've seen my brother's company build. They are making guns that fire so quickly they could take an army of soldiers down like a farmer scythes corn. Metal compartments with tracks that men can hide within. They're working on ways to deliver poisonous gases. Bombs that explode when you step on them. Bombs that can be thrown that will blow three men or more apart.' He looked up at us. 'The potential for slaughter is unimaginable.'

'I donae think I'll be working for Lord Stapleford much longer,' said Rory slowly. 'I cannae work for a murderer.'

Bertram met him with a level gaze. 'You've always known he was a murderer,' he said.

'Suspected murderer,' said Rory. 'There's never been proof. I ken it's no illegal to make arms, but I dinnae like to think that's where my wages are coming from.'

'I shouldn't feel too bad about it,' said Bertram. 'Most of the aristocracy got their money through the sacrifice of other people's blood. Slavery or industry – mills, coal pits, sites of human exploitation.'

'Excuse me,' I said, 'before we descend into

condemning all of humanity, shouldn't we do something about what is going on here and now?'

'Stop the war?' asked Bertram.

'Prevent the canal?' asked Rory.

'Find the missing woman,' I said. 'With such a contentious plan under review do you both honestly think she's simply gone missing?'

'Euphemia, we are talking about the Empire going to war!' said Bertram.

'Firstly, we don't know that is going to happen,' I said. 'We can always hope that wiser counsel will prevail. That a diplomatic solution with be found. We can always hope.' I paused, adding a silent internal prayer. 'Secondly, even if it is going to happen, I don't see there is anything any of the three of us can do about it.'

'That's because you're female,' said Rory. 'I'd be on the front line fighting for my country. Scottish or no. I'll defend Great Britain and all within with my last breath.'

Something strange happened in my chest when Rory said this. If felt like my heart fell from its moorings and dropped like a stone.

'I'd fight too,' said Bertram.

'Ye no well enough,' said Rory bluntly.

Bertram protested and went to struggle to his feet, but the effort was too much for him.

'I don't doubt the bravery of either of you,' I said firmly, 'but that is not the matter in hand. The question is, has Miss Flowers been taken by forces who want to know of this plan, or has she run off to sell the plans to a foreign power?'

'Good God,' exclaimed Bertram, 'You mean she might be a traitor! I hadn't thought of that.'

'There's rumours in the village of a German man hiding out in the woods,' I said.

'Why on earth didn't you mention this before?' barked Bertram.

'I thought it was a silly rumour,' I said defensively. 'Plus we didn't know what was going on here.'

'We knew it was a secret government meeting,' snapped Bertram.

'Oh for heaven's sake,' I said crossly. 'For all we knew it was a meeting about who was going to win the next contract for supplying army uniforms!'

'Which is likely to make someone a fortune,' said Rory. 'If you're right about what you think this canal means, Bertram.'

'When did you start calling me Bertram?' asked the man in question peevishly.

'I think when it comes to government business we're all on a fairly equal footing,' I said frankly.

'And what is that?' asked Bertram.

'Barely significant?' suggested Rory.

Bertram smiled. 'All right, but not in front of the servants or – or anyone other than Euphemia.'

'I did notice you call each other by your Christian names now,' said Rory.

'Stop getting distracted,' I commanded them. 'Mr Short gave me a letter to post a day ago. I think the German spy tried to follow me.'

'You're telling us now?' said Bertram.

'He told me it was a love letter. He'd covered it in cologne.'

'Maybe it was,' said Bertram.

Rory frowned. 'Is he rich?'

'Probably,' said Bertram.

'Och, well, maybe then.'

'But you posted it?' asked Bertram.

'I did, but what if I was sending it to a German spy?'

'Hang on, I thought you said he was in the woods?'

'That's only what a forester thinks. And what forester speaks German?' I said.

Bertram blinked and drank the rest of his glass of water down.

'I think Euphemia is simply saying that in view of this being about a secret plan for war, we need to re-examine everything that has happened,' said Rory.

'Yes, that,' I said succinctly.

'Aye, but I'm no' at all sure I don't want to scupper this plan,' said Rory. 'And if it got into the hands of the Germans that would do it.'

'That's treason!' both Bertram and I exclaimed.

'Aye, well,' said Rory looking uncomfortable and fiddling with his collar. 'Is it not treason I'd be doing if I didn't object to them tearing my country in half?'

'Treason's against the crown,' I said softly.

'Och, it's not like I can do anything,' said Rory. 'All I'm saying is if it's already happened I won't be shedding any tears over it.'

Bertram goggled at him, outraged. 'So I was right. You were behind this woman's disappearance. Did you help her leave the house?'

'Man, I've told you. All I've done is stolen a look at a few wee maps.'

'Bertram is bad enough,' said Bertram coldly. 'but I will not be addressed as "man".'

I could see Rory was about to come back with a smart comment, so I trod heavily on his foot. 'Do either of you have a way to contact Fitzroy? I have Mr Edward's number …' I trailed off.

'Let's not be hasty,' said Bertram. 'I don't want to be any more caught up with those people than I have to be.'

'Aye,' said Rory. 'On that we agree.'

'So, we should concentrate our efforts on tracing Miss Flowers,' I said. 'I can ask around in the village. I could get Susan to help. The locals are more likely to talk to her.'

'I need to get those maps back in Miss Flowers's room,' said Rory. 'I'm the quietest of all of us. I can do that.'

'And I will have a man-to-man chat this evening with Mr Short and find out if he does have an extra-marital liaison going on,' said Bertram

I must have looked shocked because Rory said, 'Did you not notice the man was wearing a wedding ring, Euphemia? It's an uncommon enough practice among men for any good servant to notice.'

'So we each have a plan of sorts.'

'I'm hoping the girl has run off with a lover she arranged to meet up here,' said Bertram. 'This could be nothing more than a silly affair.'

'I don't know that I can stand by and let the Kiel Canal go ahead,' said Rory

'What option do you have?' I said quickly. Bertram looked as if he was about to lose his temper.

Abruptly the door to Rory's parlour was wrenched open. Unable to think of anything else I jumped up and sat on the table, obscuring the maps with my person. I need not have worried. The figure in the doorway was far too distraught to notice. Eyes wide, hair in a tangle, and pale as a ghost, Merry blurted out, 'I've done a Euphemia.'

Chapter Eighteen:

The bell begins its toll

'What on earth?' exclaimed Bertram.

Rory used some choicer words that I would rather not repeat.

'She means she's found Miss Flowers's body, don't you Merry?' I said. I went forward and led her gently into the room. I noticed her arms, upper body and part of her skirts were soaked through. 'Get the fire lit,' I said to Rory, who rarely lit his own fire, thinking it an extravagance. The room was close enough to the kitchen that it never felt too chilly, but Merry was beginning to shiver with cold.

Merry turned her shocked face to me. 'I tried to get her out the water. I really did. I tried and I tried. But she was so heavy. So heavy and so cold.'

'I'd better go upstairs and tell them what's happened,' said Bertram. 'Give her some brandy, Rory. You, Euphemia, get her into some dry clothes.'

I chased Rory from the room to get Susan and lit the fire myself. Susan appeared quickly carrying a fresh uniform and some towels. Between us we got Merry undressed, dry, and dressed in fresh clothes. We had only that moment finished when Rory knocked on the door. He handed the brandy to Merry. 'You're going to need this. It sounds like the lot of them are headed downstairs.' Merry whimpered like a frightened child.

'She's in no state to be questioned,' I said.

'I'll deal with them,' said Susan unexpectedly. 'I'm not as posh as the rest of you and I can talk plain when I need to. I'll tell them we'll contact the local police and until then the girl needs to rest.'

'They may not agree,' said Rory.

'Aye, I know,' said Susan. 'That's why I'm doing it. I don't work for any of them.'

I won't deny there was chaos for quite some time, but it was perfectly true that Merry was not up to answering questions. I took her up to our room and lit the fire there too. She managed to describe where she had found the body, but then she started crying. I had never seen Merry cry before. I embraced her and rocked as I would have done little Joe. She felt thin as a bird in my arms. 'I want Merrit,' she sobbed.

Susan pulled me gently away. She held a cup of tea. 'Here, this will help with the shock,' she said and she helped Merry take a few sips. Merry quietened down. 'Now, you go to sleep and see your Merrit there,' she said. She pulled the covers up over her. Within a few moments Merry had closed her eyes and was drifting off to sleep.

'Poor wee lassie,' said Susan. 'She's got such a feisty spirit, that one, you forget what a wee scrap of a girl she is.'

'What about …'

'Oh, the men are sorted. I called the police. I'm afraid they're sending an inspector later. Bobbies coming first to take the body. Did she tell you where it is?' I nodded. 'The Big Man's been on the phone to London for a long while. Now they're all closeted upstairs. I'd lay my bets they'll be asking for their luncheon soon.'

'You're joking,' I said.

'Yon English are not ones for missing their meals,' said Susan contemptuously. 'And you better look about yourself quick smart. You've your duties and Merry's now to cover.'

Sure enough luncheon had been ordered. Afterwards the men moved through to the library for coffee while we waited for the police to appear.

'Do you think I should go and sit with the body,' I said as I did the washing up.

'I don't know,' said Susan. 'I don't like to think of her out there alone.'

'Under the circumstances I don't think I would consider it safe for Euphemia to go out there alone,' said Rory.

'I'll go,' said Jock, surprising us all. 'If there's someone out there murdering women, me and my cleaver would like a wee word.'

'We don't know –' I began.

'I think that's a grand idea, Jock,' said Rory. 'Thank you.'

'It's nothing, man,' muttered the big chef.

Susan stood on tiptoe to kiss him on the cheek. 'Ye kind soul, you,' she said. Jock blushed, brushed us all aside, and stomped off into the countryside, cleaver in hand.

'I hope he doesn't meet any tinkers,' said Susan darkly. 'Jock doesn't like tinkers. Not since one of them ruined his best knife.'

Bertram appeared at the baize door. 'A word, Euphemia?'

He took me to a quiet corner. 'I've had a word with Mr Short. A man-to-man sort of thing. Pointed out the police would be enquiring and all that.' He blushed slightly, 'The long and the short of it is that the man does fancy himself as a bit of a Casanova. In fact once I'd got him going on his conquests it was damn hard to stop him.' He took a handkerchief from his pocket and mopped his suddenly sweaty brow. 'I'm happy to believe it was a love letter he got you to send. He brought it up. Said as you were from Stapleford could I get you to hush up about it. I said I would.'

'What?'

'Be realistic, Euphemia. Even if the girl was murdered the police aren't going to get far with this, are they?' He paused, sighed at my slowness and said, 'A few telephone calls here, a few telephone calls there, and that ministry man will close the investigation down.'

'But that's wrong.'

'Safety of the realm and all that,' said Bertram. 'It's not as if anyone seems to have liked her much.'

'But … but …'

'I know. I feel the same,' said Bertram. 'I'm going to stay up tonight and do some drinking with the other gentlemen. I've been avoiding that, but I'll say I feel it's my duty as a host to do something special under the circumstances tonight. Keep our spirits up. I'll get out some of the best wines and see if I can't get a few tongues wagging.'

'You mean you'll investigate?' I said.

Bertram gave me a lop-sided smile. 'Isn't that what we do best, Euphemia? Mind you, I'm still going to be hoping it was a silly accident.'

'What about Rory?' I asked.

'He's in a difficult position with this Kiel Canal thing. It might be fairer not to get him involved at this stage.'

'I agree,' I said, knowing I was taking the easy way out.

'Is Merry all right?'

'She's sleeping like a baby. Must be the shock. It really knocked the stuffing out of her.'

Bertram placed a hand on my arm. 'She'll be fine. Our Merry is made of stern stuff.'

A team of two local bobbies led by a much subdued Constable McClintock arrived a few hours later. It seemed the reality of a dead female body and having to deal with it had poured cold water over his enthusiasm. I was about to describe where she was, when he interrupted me. 'I ken you've duties in the house, Miss St John, but we'd all feel more comfortable if you would accompany us. None of us feel right about manhandling a female. Being kirk-goers like.'

I was on the point of saying that I thought this was unnecessary under the circumstances when he added, 'Please, miss. I'm sorry about last night. I ken I got a wee bit carried away, but none of us has even seen a dead body before. The village midwife deals with the dead, but we've orders to carry the body to Doc Stuart's house. There's folk saying the police might ask him to cut her up. They've strong feelings about that sort of thing up here. We don't do it.'

'You're thinking if I'm with you there would be less likelihood of trouble.'

Constable McClintock gave a small smile and suddenly looked very young. 'We've been told Jock's up there with his cleaver. I reckon if we have someone like you from the Lodge with us, we've covered most angles.'

I told Susan. She wasn't happy with my going, but Rory took off his jacket and offered to muck in with the cleaning up in the kitchen and if need be the dinner if Jock wasn't back in time. Susan was so taken aback at the idea of a butler cooking that she raised no more objections.

I led the little band through the woods. We found Jock sitting on the bank looking mournful. He'd dragged the body out of the loch and covered it with an old tarpaulin he'd brought with him. 'I wouldn't go looking under that, Euphemia,' he said. 'Fish have been at her.' At this point one of the younger bobbies bolted into the forest and we heard him all too clearly reacquainting himself with his dinner.[14] McClintock had gone paler, but he and the other bobby were manfully trying to hold themselves together.

'It's all right, laddie,' said Jock. 'I've rolled her in tight in yon tarp. Yer willnae need to see her. Even the coffin maker won't need to undo it. I take it it's Fraser will be doing it?'

'We have to take her to Dr Stuart,' said McClintock.

'I can assure you she's verra died,' said Jock.

'The police asked …' McClintock trailed off.

'You're the police,' said Jock.

'We've an inspector coming up.'

Jock heaved a big sigh. 'Do whatever you have to, laddie, but if no one will be sitting with the lady tonight at least get the doctor to light a candle.'

'Aye,' said McClintock. 'Aye, I'll do that, Jock. And thank ye,' he gestured to the body. 'Thank ye for doing that.'

'I'm an old soldier, laddie,' said Jock, taking me quite my surprise. 'I've seen worse on the battlefield. At least yon lassie was dead when the fish began their meal. From what I could see from what was left of her face she looked verra peaceful.'

This was too much for McClintock and his other companion. They both bolted into the woods. We soon

---

[14]Dinner being the midday meal the ordinary folk round here took.

heard them being overcome with the same malady as their fellow.

Jock looked at me. 'Strong stomach,' he said approvingly.

'My father was a vicar,' I said. 'I'm no stranger to being around the dead. Though I am very grateful you covered her poor face.'

'I didnae take to her much meself, but it's always a sadness when the young get taken. Have they told her poor parents?'

'I don't know,' I said. I hadn't thought about Miss Flowers having a mother or father. Suddenly I felt a wave of pity for them and their daughter. Tears started to my eyes.

Jock heaved his bulk to his feet. 'I'll be going and getting the wee laddies. Then we can get this poor lassie inside.'

I admit at that point I shed a few tears, but I don't feel any the worse for that. I think it is right that we cry over the dead. It's a form of tribute to them. My father used to say grief is nature's (and God's) way of reminding us not to take the living for granted and for appreciating what the dead did for us. Miss Flowers hadn't done anything for me, but it's rare to find a human being in this world who is loved by no one, even if it is only their mother. We're all babes once, and babes are loved and looked on as signs of hope and future joy. Sometimes how we lead and end our lives does not live up to those early hopes, but once we all had that potential – or so I believe, and when it comes to a sudden end like this it is always a tragedy.

The pale-faced constables got Miss Flowers safely to Dr Stuart's home, who promised that he would indeed light a candle. By the time Jock and I got back to the Lodge it was well past time for dinner, so Rory must have managed something. Lights were burning in the library and there was the sound of loud male conversation, so I assumed Bertram had gone through with this plan. Susan was nowhere to be found, so refusing Jock's offer of an omelette I took myself off to bed. If the men needed anything further Rory would have to manage again. My day had already been too full.

That night I dreamt of rows of young men marching through fog. As the mist swirled I saw they wore army uniforms and even in the dream I wept to think of the war that might be coming. But when they reached me they passed straight through my body. Then I realised they were not marching off to war. They were ghosts heading rank after rank into the darkness.

Chapter Nineteen:

An inspector calls

I woke slightly before dawn. Despite the coldness of the room, my body dripped with perspiration. Blood pounded in my ears. I knew I had to remember if I had seen Rory's face among the dead. The grey light that peeked through the curtains thinned, but images from that dream hung around me like veils or clouds. I could see Merry stirring in the other bed, but I could also still see the ranks of men marching past me into the receding night.

I must have spoken aloud without realising it for Merry suddenly appeared at my side. 'Wake up! You're having a nightmare,' she said.

'I'm not asleep,' I replied. 'I can see you, Merry. And I can see them, so many of them, passing me into death. I have to watch. I have to see if Rory is there.'

At least I think that's what I said. These were certainly the words I formed in my mind. I saw confusion cross Merry's face. Then resolution. The next moment I was soaked and gasping. She'd emptied the wash basin over me. I sat up among my sodden blankets, spluttering for breath and furious.

'Has it gone?' asked Merry cautiously from the other side of the room.

'What?'

'The night terror. Has it gone?'

I was about to ask her, quite crudely, what she was talking about when I realised the faces of the dead were gone. I also found I could not recall if Rory had been among them. I burst into tears.

'Gawd almighty,' said Merry, coming over and gingerly giving me a hug. 'I was the one that discovered the bleedin' body.'

I pushed her gently away and stripped off my wet nightclothes. The grey had totally gone from the new day and I knew we both had duties to attend to. 'Let's get on with things,' I said. 'I don't know about you, but I need to feel I'm doing something normal.'

'It's this place,' muttered Merry, pulling on her uniform. 'Every time we come up here something terrible happens.'

No, I thought, it's not the place. It's what we bring with us, but I didn't share this thought with Merry. If she thought that when we left the Highlands we'd leave all this behind then I wanted her to go on thinking that as long as possible. After last night I had no doubt that death stalked me and it would not be long before it stalked us all.

You can tell, I imagine, that I did not dispense coffee and tea in the breakfast room with the brightest of smiles.

The atmosphere in the kitchen had been sober. Susan and Jock had barely exchanged a word. But the atmosphere in the breakfast room was something else. Bertram spent much of breakfast holding his head in his hands and groaning softly. Rory was coldly reserved. Mr Nose, Mr Beard, and Mr Bald ate little and what they did eat was interrupted frequently by one of them suddenly whispering urgently and the others pushing their heads so close together they almost touched. The whole thing reminded me of some kind of human tortoise that was occasionally poking its head and limbs out of its shell and

131

then withdrawing again. Merry's eyes were wide with wonder at the performance. 'What are they doing?' she mouthed to me as she tried to dodge between them and their actions to remove the dirty plates. I had a little more experience of this sort of behaviour, so I was able to mouth back, 'Hung over.' Merry gave a little giggle which she had to stifle quickly when Rory shot her a furious look.

It was fortunate that we had not only loaded the dirty dishes into the dumb waiter, but also dispensed the coffee cups before the rest of the party joined us. My back was to the door when it opened. I was offering coffee from a silver pot to Mr Nose. Merry was meant to be pouring tea for Bertram, but she looked up when the door opened and poured the greater part of it on the floor. Bertram, head still in hands, did not notice and most surprising of all Rory, that most professional of butlers, looked shocked at the sight of whatever stood in the door way. It took an extreme effort of will for me not to turn round.

When the two gentlemen, Mr Ministry and Mr Short, passed me, I saw nothing amiss. However when they seated themselves at the table I saw that Mr Ministry sported a wide, barely scabbed cut along his left cheekbone and Mr Short had a spectacular black eye of the sort rarely seen in anyone aged over eleven.

Merry stopped pouring tea on the floor. A quick glance at Rory told her she had got away with it.

'Would you like me to fetch some fresh steak from the kitchen for your eye, Mr Sh-Smith?' she asked in a totally expressionless voice. At that moment the doorbell rang and Rory was forced to subtly excuse himself.

He returned a few moments later and whispered in Mr Ministry's ear. I wasn't close enough to hear what was said, but I could swear I saw a moment of distress cross the seated man's face, but it was gone as soon as it has appeared and the government man was back to an impassivity that rivalled Rory's.

Mr Ministry said aloud, 'Thank you. We should prefer to be left alone now.'

'I will clear the cups for you, sir.'

'No, go now,' said the other man sharply.

Rory made an irritated ushering motion with his hands at me that was both entirely unnecessary and offensive. Bertram appeared to be aware of nothing but his hangover.

Back in the kitchen, I turned on Rory, 'You don't have to shoo me out of a room like a stray dog!'

'Might I remind you, Euphemia, that at this time you are a maid and that is no way to speak to the butler of your household.'

'Oh, pah!' I said and gave a loud and unladylike snort that would have made my mother faint.

'Who was at the door,' asked the practical Merry.

'An Inspector Walker,' said Rory. 'I imagine he will want to speak with us all in due course. Purely as a matter of routine,' he added seeing Merry beginning to frown. 'The Inspector has taken up residence in the library. Perhaps you could get one of your girls, Mrs Simpson, to take him and his sergeant a cup of tea.'

'It's still early,' said Jock. 'Do you think they'll fancy a wee bit of breakfast. Got to be nasty working on this case.'

'An hospitable thought, Jock,' said Rory. 'I think in the first instance we should send the tea and enquire if they would like further refreshment.'

'Yes,' said Merry, 'it'd be kind of difficult interviewing someone with your mouth full of bacon sarnie.'

Rory frowned down at her, but Merry merely shrugged and set about making the tea. Rory retired to his parlour.

'What's got into yon mannie?' asked Jock, who I felt was becoming quite the conversationalist. Or maybe he was finally warming to us folk from 'down south'.

'I think he had quite a rough night with the gentlemen last night,' said Susan. 'He told me he didn't get to his own bed till past 4 a.m. He also seemed to take it badly that you'd gone off to show the police where the poor woman was, Euphemia.'

I shrugged.

'What kept him up so late?' asked Merry over the kettle's whistle.

'I've told you a thousand times, Merry,' said Susan. 'You dinnae let the water boil for tea. It doesnae taste the same.'

Merry gave me a look behind Susan's back that couldn't have more clearly said that she didn't care.

'It seems your Mr Stapleford gave a wee party,' said Jock. 'And it all got a wee bittie out of hand.'

'Oooh! That sounds interesting,' said Merry.

'Take the tea up, Merry,' said Susan firmly. My curiosity had also been awoken. But first while the gentleman divided their time between finishing their breakfast and seeing the Inspector I decided I would go and tidy their bedrooms. This task was usually either undertaken by both Merry and I. We would work on these rooms together as an issue of personal safety in case any of the gentlemen acquired ideas. Not that this group seemed to be up to the kind of 'doings' that can happen above stairs. It had meant, however, that I had never had a proper chance to search any of the rooms. Merry was scrupulous in not going through any guest's belongings. She might have a natural inquisitiveness, but she was utterly honest and despite the many shortcomings of Stapleford House would never have taken as much as a pin. She had never even read Richenda's diaries when she had the chance.

I also like to think I would have been honest enough not to delve into private possessions normally, but to my detriment I knew when acts as despicable as murder came into play one could not play by the normal rules that one has been taught.

I started by going through Mr Short's room. The first object that caught my eye was an enormous bottle of cologne. I knew from the letter he had sent that he possessed such a thing, but it had not before been placed out among his possessions. A briefcase stood, partly concealed by a curtain, but it was securely locked. A quick glance into the corridor showed me no sign of Merry or anyone else. I started to go through the drawers on his dresser. I found the usual socks, handkerchiefs, cufflinks, and a most unusual box that contained an ingenious opening mechanism that took me some moments to open. When I did I was disappointed to see it contained several rolled-up sections of rubber. These appeared to be covered in talcum powder. I chose not to unroll them as the fit in the box was very snug. I couldn't conceive of what use these would be, but neither could I see how they could harm anyone. The last item I uncovered of any note was a small box that contained spare cards for Mr Short's card case. I learned his name was Harold Leech and he was a director of a construction company. Rory, Bertram, and I had been right about the nature of the house gathering.

I had just shut the lid of the box and was sliding it back between the socks where it had been kept, when Merry opened the door. Seeing me with my hands deep in a gentleman's drawers brought an expression of shock and outrage to her face.

'It's not what it looks like,' I protested.

Chapter Twenty:

Accusations and recriminations abound

Merry refused to discuss the situation. We continued to work through the bedrooms in turn. I felt her eyes on me as I worked alongside her, so I didn't so much as attempt to place a hair on my head where it shouldn't be. I did try to do a visual search of each room, but even this was difficult with Merry watching me like a hawk. The only things I noticed were that Mr Bald had extremely large feet and kept a hairbrush on his dresser. I shuddered to think what he might do with it. All four of the other men had pictures of their families on display. Mr Short had a young wife and two small children of indeterminate sex on display. Mr Nose had a wife nearly his own age, but who was still extremely pretty, and three small boys. Mr Beard appeared to have two grown-up sons, but the picture of his wife was edged in black, so I assumed he was a widower. Mr Ministry had a beautiful young wife and four children of varying ages that she was surely too young to have borne. A second wife, I guessed.

When we had finished and were on the way back down the servants' stair, Merry paused halfway. 'I ain't going to tell Rory or Susan what I saw, but I'll be watching you and if I see anything suspicious I'll go right to them.'

'Merry, we've known each other for years. You can't believe I'm a thief.'

'I know what I saw,' said Merry firmly. Her face softened slightly. 'I don't believe in the normal way of things you'd be tempted, but Gawd knows you've been through a lot. I'm putting it down to a mental fit of some kind. I'm only watching you for your own good.'

I struggled internally and then said meekly, 'Thank you, Merry. It won't happen again.'

'Course it won't,' said Merry and gave me a quick hug. We separated at the entrance to the kitchen. I took myself off to Rory's parlour.

'Merry thinks I'm a thief,' as I walked through the door without knocking. I then proceeded to explain to Rory, who had been ironing the paper, it arrived very late in the Highlands, what had happened.

'So it is all about the Kiel Canal,' said Rory dourly.

'Yes,' I said, 'but what am I going to do about Merry? I can't tell her what we are really up to.'

Rory's face darkened, 'Did you put Bertram up to that ridiculous party last night?'

'No, it was entirely his own idea. He thought tongues might be loosed with the addition of some of Richard's good wine.'

'I hope he is satisfied with the results.'

'What happened?'

'What didn't,' said Rory sourly. 'The one Merry called Mr Beard spent much of the night weeping and lamenting.'

'He's a widower,' I said.

'Of recent date, I would hazard to guess,' said Rory. 'The man has my sympathy, but it's very difficult for a butler to know what to do when a man collapses weeping in front of him.'

'What did you do?'

'I pretended not to see his distress and fetched him a

cup of cocoa.'

'A solution,' I said.

'Hmm,' said Rory, 'but I was close to weeping myself when Bertram started to sing and do impressions of chorus girls. Apparently, due to his small stature, he often played the female role in his school plays.'

I stored this image away for future perusal at a happier time. 'He must have been very drunk.'

'Hmm,' said Rory, 'and I hope I'm as broad-minded as the next man, but the stories your Mr Short told could even have curled Mr Bald's hair.'

'What?'

'Lewd,' said Rory. 'Unrepeatable in your presence.'

I shrugged. 'Gentleman.'

'There was nothing gentle about any of these men. And as for the fight in the garden, it was at that point I informed Bertram of my desire to quit Richard Stapleford's employ and retired to my bedchamber.'

'Who fought who?' I asked.

'To my eyes it appeared to be a general scrum,' said Rory. 'I note that you have no remarked on my resignation.'

'I assumed it was given in the heat of the moment. These guests obviously went far beyond what it was reasonable to ask you to deal with. I'm sure Bertram will realise you didn't mean it.'

'But I did,' said Rory. 'I most certainly did.'

A knock at the door interrupted us. Merry poked her head in. 'Inspector Walker would like to see Miss St John now,' she said.

'You'd better go,' said Rory. 'The sooner this is all over. The sooner – well, it's over.' Merry gave us both an odd look. I left without another word.

Mr Walker was seated in one of the wing-back chairs

by the fire. His sergeant, a neat, black-haired man of medium height, stood behind him notebook at the ready. A straight-backed wooden chair had been placed for me. It did not look comfortable.

Inspector Walker, from the top of his perfectly cut short blond hair to his highly polished brogues, was a model of style and decorum. His suit fitted him perfectly and looked to be beyond the price the average policeman could afford. When he spoke his accent clearly showed he came from the upper classes. I didn't doubt he was a policeman, but I suspected he had been carefully selected for this case.

'Please be seated, Miss St John,' he said, indicating the chair. 'I understand you led the men to where the body was found.'

I waited for his question. Inspector Walker said nothing, but regarded me with clear, grey eyes. Was he waiting for me to confess? The thought flitted across my mind and I dismissed it as ridiculous. I waited.

The inspector turned and spoke in a low voice to his sergeant, who scribbled something in his notebook. I repressed an urge to fidget. Honestly, sometimes I was grateful for my mother's training.

After what felt like an age Inspector Walker asked, 'How did you know where the body was?'

'Merry – I mean Mary – the maid told me where she had found it.'

'And you recognised the spot immediately despite not being a native of the area?'

'A loch is a large body of water and difficult to miss.' I bit the edge of my tongue. Why did I feel so on edge?

'Indeed,' said Walker smoothly, 'and has a correspondingly large circumference. By that I mean …'

'I know what you mean,' I interrupted, 'but despite her shock Merry was very clear where she had been. I have also had occasion to visit this Lodge before.'

'There was also your rather fraught trip through the countryside when you met a monster, I believe?' He arched an eyebrow at this. 'Or was it the German spy?'

'I was certainly followed by someone,' I said, 'and I confess the experience did alarm me. I may have been prey to some ridiculous imaginings.'

'You don't strike me as the kind of girl prone to fits of hysteria,' said Walker, 'but then perhaps you were under some pressure from other things?'

'I have no idea what you mean,' I said coldly.

'I mean,' said Mr Walker leaning forward and speaking in friendly conversational tone, 'the murder of Miss Flowers.'

I started in my chair almost knocking it over. 'You can't be serious,' I said.

Mr Walker leaned back in his chair. 'My friends tell me I have absolutely no sense of humour,' he said.

'Why on earth would I want to harm Miss Flowers?'

'The very question I asked myself,' said Walker.

'And what answer did you give yourself?' My voice sounded waspish even to my own ears.

'Well, the lady in question was, as I understand, one who had dragged herself up out of her social class. Whereas you have obviously fallen. So jealousy may have been an issue.'

I did not like that he had pinpointed my class so easily. 'Hardly enough,' I said.

Mr Walker cocked his head to one side. 'Perhaps, but circumstances can bring certain emotions to the boil. Such as the lady in question treating you in a demeaning manner and even threatening to have your best friend fired.'

'Which didn't happen,' I pointed out.

Mr Walker continued as if I had not spoken. 'And then

there is the question of the affair the butler, McLeod, isn't it? Was having with the deceased.' He paused. 'And the one he broke off with you.'

'How dare you!' I exclaimed, rising to my feet. 'Mr McLeod was not involved with Miss Flowers.'

'Maybe. Maybe not. But there was a time when you certainly believed that to be the case. It all adds up to a most plausible motive, don't you agree, Sergeant?'

'In my experience a jilted female is a dangerous creature,' said the sergeant.

'You have much experience with them, do you, Sergeant?' I said in what I hoped was a coldly condescending voice.

'Indeed, miss,' he replied, 'I've not long finished a case where such a woman proved to be at the heart of it. Hanging next week, she is.'

Chapter Twenty-one:

Desperate times

Jock thrust a mug of tea into my hand. For once I drank the overly strong brew without protest. 'Accused you of the murder, did he?' he asked.

I nodded. I didn't trust myself to speak without bursting into tears.

'Did the same to all of us,' said Jock. 'Me, Susan, Merry and McLeod. No idea how he treated 'em upstairs, but he certainly gave us a going over.' He chuckled.

'You too?' I gasped.

'Aye, it's a grand technique. Closes his cases verra quickly. Lots of confessions. He made a good case for me certainly. If I'd done it I might well have cracked.'

'But the things he knew about me.'

'Man does his homework,' said Jock in a voice of respect.

'He reminded me of those folks you get at the fayres sometimes,' said Merry. I looked at her quizzically. 'You know the ones that pretend to tell your fortune and seem to know everything about you. It's all a trick. They actually get the stuff from you, but in a way you don't notice.'

I shook my head. 'No, he definitely knew things about me I didn't tell him.'

Susan shrugged. 'Then someone must have told him. Now look sharp – we need to get the luncheon served inspector or no inspector.'

'Will he eat with them?' asked Merry.

'No, he will not,' said Rory, appearing in the doorway. 'The *inspector*,' and he said the word with obvious distaste, 'will take a cold luncheon in the library with his sergeant. There is no need to prepare anything special, Jock.'

'Aye, right,' said Jock with a grin.

The day progressed with a dull mundanity that was at odds with the true situation. Not until late afternoon did I get a chance to speak with Bertram. He came into the kitchen wearing his coat and made what he fondly thought were discreet signals that I should meet him outside. Fortunately only Jock was in the kitchen with me at the time and all his concentration was on his clear soup for dinner, which was currently looking sadly speckled.

Bertram stood hopping from one foot to another in the kitchen garden. He had a tweed cap on his head and had let down the ears so it covered the greater part of his terrible beard. 'Let's go into the forest,' he said, taking my arm.

'If we must,' I said.

Bertram kept up a smart pace until we were out of sight of the house. 'That bloody inspector accused me of murdering Miss Flowers!' he exclaimed.

'He accused all the staff too. Though I'm surprised he tried the same tactic with you.'

'He suggested I was having a liaison with the woman.' Bertram shuddered dramatically.

'You didn't tell him anything about my history with Rory, did you, Bertram?'

'Good Lord, Euphemia, I'm not a sneak!' He paused. 'That gets beaten out of you at school.'

I gave a slight smile. 'What do you think happened to her?'

'Well, if it hadn't been for the maps you found in her room I'd think the silly woman died of the cold. Getting into a loch in winter!'

'Does the inspector know about the maps?' I asked.

'Unless you told him, I suspect not.'

'Should I tell him?'

'He'd only want to know why you were snooping. Besides, the maps are probably covered by the Official Secrets Act.' He scratched under the cap's ears. 'By the way, in case you thinking of mentioning it telling someone you've signed the official secrets act is also not allowed under the act.'

'That's ridiculous. That means there's a whole line of enquiry the inspector can't follow unless he's signed it too.'

'And we can't ask him,' said Bertram. 'But to be honest, although he's obviously been briefed that there was some kind of meeting going on here, he's been very careful not to ask questions about what has been discussed. If he'd signed he wouldn't have that issue, so I don't think he has.'

'But if she was killed because of the maps?'

'I'm not sure how that would work,' said Bertram. 'I agree it's likely she was sharing or selling information that she shouldn't have been, but how did that get her killed? If Mr Ministry had figured that out he'd have more than enough resources to have her carted away somewhere.'

'Maybe she was threatening to expose the person she'd been giving the information to and they killed her.'

Bertram shook his head. 'But that would mean giving herself away as well.'

'So maybe it was death by misadventure,' I said.

'Doesn't feel like it though, does it?' said Bertram. 'We've been in enough of these situations to tell when something feels funny.'

I sighed. 'I agree, but my most likely suspect is Rory trying to scupper the Kiel Canal plan.'

Bertram put his finger quickly to my lips. He looked around frantically. 'Sssh,' he said urgently.

I couldn't help recalling he had been scratching his beard with that hand. I removed the finger. 'I don't think he did.'

'Not that,' said Bertram irritably. 'You mustn't mention … mention … the water thing. We weren't meant to know about that. Don't know that knowing about it doesn't count as treason.'

'Oh, damn Fitzroy,' I said.

'Euphemia!' said Bertram, obviously shocked.

'He sent us into a situation where we had no idea what was going on.'

'I think that was the idea,' said Bertram gloomily. 'I think he hoped we'd obediently not ask questions and behave docilely.'

'Doesn't know us, does he?'

Bertram grinned. 'No. But I am concerned about Rory. Not that he's killed anyone, but that he might do something drastic.'

'They wouldn't really do it, would they?' I asked. 'It seems like a daft idea to me.'

Bertram's eyes gleamed. 'It would be an incredible feat of engineering. If it weren't for the consequences I'd love to see it done.' He shrugged. 'But no, I don't see how the government could afford it and afford to build the ships. Seems to me their choice is between a new fleet and this thing.'

'You should explain that to Rory.'

'I would but I'm not in his best books at the moment. He's still talking about resigning.'

'Well, he's not talking to me either.'

'Drat it,' said Bertram. 'We need the three of us to work this one out. If that inspector keeps digging around I don't know I trust Rory to keep his mouth shut.'

'What happened last night? Who fought and why?'

'Oh, Mr Short said something unsavoury about Mr Ministry's wife.'

'What?'

'Oh I don't know, Euphemia. We were all pretty drunk by then. Besides even if I did I couldn't tell you. You being a female.'

'What are we going to do?' I asked.

'What can we do?' said Bertram. 'I'm glad to hear the wretched man is accusing everyone. I can tell you I was worried for a bit. No, now we just have to keep calm, say as little as possible and keep our eyes open. Something has to turn up.'

'I hope so,' I said solemnly. 'I think you're right. If Inspector Walker keeps probing things are going to get a great deal worse.'

'Damn Fitzroy,' seconded Bertram. We trudged silently side by side back to the house. We separated as I made for the kitchen door and Bertram let himself in through the front.

I'd barely closed the door behind me before Susan was on me. 'What's this nonsense about Mr McLeod resigning? I can't manage without him! Even if we managed to serve meals and I set Merry to answering the door – and it's only the police liable to be calling – who can I send to deliver sir's night-time drink? He's most insistent he has one before bed.'

'Why?' I asked.

'He said he doesn't sleep well. He needs something to take his sleeping powder with.'

And then, of course, I knew. The only question was how on earth would I prove it? The first scheme that flashed through my mind was incredibly dangerous. There had to be another way, didn't there?

'Rory won't leave until he's handed Richard Stapleford his resignation, Susan,' I said distractedly.

'Oh. It's that Mr Walker. He's got me all wound up.'

Inspector Walker? It had to be worth a shot.

Chapter Twenty-two:

In which Euphemia makes a case

Inspector Walker was between interviewees. He was indulging in a fish-paste sandwich when I entered the library without knocking.

'I don't believe I asked to see you, Miss St John,' he said calmly. 'But anything that takes my attention away from this terrible sandwich is most welcome.' He put the sandwich down. 'I don't think your cook likes me.'

'I imagine he didn't like being accused of murder,' I said tartly.

Inspector Walker smiled slightly. 'You'd be surprised how much people reveal when they are accused.'

'I'm sure,' I said. 'But I know who did it.'

'So what makes you think this is a murder case?

'Other than your presence?' I said.

'May I say that you are one of the most unusual maids I have ever come across? Please take a seat and tell me all about yourself.'

I sat down. 'The man from the Ministry did it.'

'Mr Fairchild?'

'Probably,' I said cautiously and described the man in question.

'That's Arthur Fairchild,' said Inspector Walker, 'but I am a little troubled that you would accuse a man without even knowing his name. It doesn't sound as if you've done your research properly.'

'We weren't given any of the guests' names. In view of the nature of the meeting ...' I stopped in time.

The Inspector raised an eyebrow. 'You know what the meeting is about? Even I haven't been allowed to know that.'

I wriggled uncomfortably in my seat. 'I can't tell you.'

'Miss St John, can you give me a single reason why I shouldn't discount anything you tell me as the fantasies of an obviously intelligent and bored household maid? I don't know what led you to take a position far below your obvious station, but while I might sympathise with your situation I can always arrest you for wasting police time and for defamation of character.'

I leant forward. 'Listen,' I said in a firm voice, 'this is a highly secret government meeting yet Mr Fairchild brings his secretary. Ask anyone, she didn't strike one as someone to be trusted with government secrets. Then there's Mr Leech, who is a known womaniser.'

'I thought you didn't know any of their names?'

I ignored him and carried on. 'If you consider Mr Fairchild's wife, obviously his second wife, he has a predilection for young women. Mr Fairchild and Mr Leech got into a fight, which I believe was about Miss Flowers's affections.'

'After she had disappeared.'

'He would still be angry about Mr Leech's affair with her.'

'Because he was having an affair with her himself?'

'Yes, and every night he takes a sleeping pill to help him sleep.'

'How does that fit with midnight trysts?'

'Oh, he wasn't doing anything here,' I said blushing furiously. 'He brought her with him so he could keep an eye on her. He's a very jealous man and she is – was – a flighty sort of girl.' The inspector made to speak again, but I rushed on, 'But the final nail in his coffin is what Jock said about the girl's body. He said despite the state of it she had a peaceful look on her face, as if she'd fallen asleep.'

'So you think Mr Fairchild slipped her some sleeping pills before she went out to the loch and she was overcome when she was in the water?'

'Yes.'

'Wouldn't he have had to time that with the precision of a chemist?'

'I don't know,' I said. 'He would know how long it took the pills to affect him. Maybe he gave them to her before she left the house hoping she'd be overcome in the forest and he …'

'Could dispose of the body?' finished the Inspector.

'Exactly,' I said, sitting back in my seat. 'So you see how he did it?'

'I think it is a most entertaining theory,' said the inspector. 'I also think I must ask you never to repeat this. You have not one shred of evidence. Nothing a case could be built on. I think, young lady, you should leave murder to the professionals. I can overlook this one indiscretion, but spreading malicious stories like this is beneath you and illegal.'

'I thought you could find the evidence,' I protested.

'That isn't how police procedure works,' said the inspector. 'Now I suggest you return to your duties and leave me to get on with my job.' He paused, 'Unless there is anything else you could add that would lend credibility to your story.'

Of course, there was, but I couldn't tell him any of it. So I shook my head. The inspector gave a meaningful look at the door. I got up and left. My face was flaming and I was shaking slightly. 'Damn Fitzroy,' I exploded as the door closed behind me. Fortunately there was no one in the corridor. There was nothing else for it. I was going to have to proceed with my plan. It was the only way I could imagine justice being done, but it would be so dangerous I couldn't ask anyone, even Bertram, to help me. I also had to put it into action as soon as possible. And that meant that night.

My first task was to sneak into Miss Flowers's room. The inspector and sergeant seemed permanently fixed in the library, so before my nerve broke I went straight to the dead woman's bedroom. To my relief and surprise, the small satchel of maps still rested under the mattress. I might have been able to make my plan work without them, but this helped a great deal. I could only assume that Rory had replaced the maps after the room had been searched, or that whoever had searched it wasn't that good at their job. Certainly it had been placed far enough under the mattress that Merry making the beds hadn't found it. Or perhaps she had and simply left it there.

I took the satchel, and rather than taking it back to my room I hid it in one the bookcases on the corridor behind books I thought it unlikely anyone present would read – a three-part edition of Shakespeare's plays.

The rest of the staff would be sitting down to an early supper soon before we served the guests. I would have liked to have found an actual prop, but seeing as I wasn't going to give it to Mr Fairchild, I simply went back and rummaged around the room a bit longer, checking the patterns on Miss Flowers's make-up case, her luggage, and other small personal items. I learned she was a lover of floral designs. Indeed her perfume was a sickly violet and rose affair. I sprayed it in the air and took note of the primary notes that a man might notice. A woman would only have said sickly and sweet, but to an infatuated man I imagined it smelled like summer and walking in an ornamental garden.

No one saw me do any of this. I then hurried down to dinner, explaining I had been lying down due to a bad headache. Susan and Merry were most sympathetic, Merry observing how 'peaky' I looked. I struggled to eat my meal and this led to everyone being most concerned. I did not tell them my lost appetite had nothing to do with my imaginary headache, but that I was almost overcome with nausea. Indeed, I had the sense to be terrified about what I must do that very night. I had no way of knowing if I would survive.

Chapter Twenty-three:

Playing the game

I had no intention of prowling the corridors late into the night. Rather, the more people who were awake when I instigated my plan, the safer I would be. So while the gentlemen were sipping their port, I slipped away and picked up the satchel. I positioned myself outside the dining room door, partially concealed by a small alcove.

At last the door to the dining room opened. I was in luck. Mr Fairchild came out first. I stepped forward and allowed him to see the satchel I was holding. As I had hoped, he recognised it at once. Proving he had been promoted for his brains and not his connections, he turned in the doorway and said loudly to the others that he wanted to have a look at something in the gun room and would join them in the library later.

This was certainly not the room I would have chosen for our confrontation, but I took his meaning and hurried down there. A cool twenty minutes later, during which time I had been tempted to abandon my plan more times than I had breathed out, Mr Arthur Fairchild walked slowly into the room, carrying a glass and swirling his brandy. He came in and shut the door. Then he turned the key in the lock and pocketed it. I could have kicked myself. It would have been the simplest thing for me to have removed the key before he arrived. Now I was trapped in here with him. I would need to make this good.

Mr Fairchild sat down in the one comfortable seat, crossed one leg lazily over the other and drawled, 'So?'

'You recognised the satchel?' I said. I didn't add 'sir'. I didn't want to give him any advantage he did not already have.

'It belonged to my secretary, Miss Flowers. If you give it to me I shall see it is returned to her family and no more questions will be asked. If not ….' The threat lingered in the air.

'You have just removed any doubts I had of your innocence,' I said coolly. I opened the satchel and laid out the maps on the gun-cleaning table.

Fairchild shot out of seat. 'How the devil do you have these?' he cried. 'This is top secret government business.'

'Oh don't worry,' I said calmly. 'I have signed the Official Secrets Act.'

Fairchild picked up one the maps, frowned over it and then began to fold and gather all the maps. I made no move to stop him. 'So you work for us?' he said.

'Loosely speaking,' I confirmed.

Fairchild sat back down clutching the maps. 'I didn't think we'd been sent here without some kind of security,' he said. 'But a maid. My goodness. This *is* the new century.' He took a few deep breaths. 'I have to thank you. Obviously Miss Flowers took advantage of her position.'

'You had no idea?' I asked.

'None,' said Fairchild, shaking his head slowly. It was said with sincerity and I believed him.

'So it wasn't a misplaced sense of honour that made you kill her?' I asked.

'What on earth are you talking about?'

'The sleeping pills in her morning tea. They overcame her when she was in the water and she drowned. I imagine you were pleased about that. The pills would have killed her anyway, but her drowning was so much easier than you having to comb the woods to hide the body. It couldn't have worked out better, could it?'

'I don't know what you're talking about,' said Fairchild again, but the colour had gone from his face.

'The satchel wasn't all I found. Miss Flowers seems to have been a little indiscreet. Or maybe she was hoping to protect herself.'

Fairchild got up. 'I don't need to listen to any more of this nonsense.' He moved towards the door and began to fumble for the key.

'She kept a journal. A pretty little flowery book. It smells of roses. I assume that was her favourite scent. Perhaps you even bought it for her.' I gave what I hoped was a dramatic pause and then said, 'She wrote about your affair in some detail.'

At this every line in Fairchild's body stiffened. He stayed frozen for a moment. Then slowly he turned around. The look on his face was a mixture of fear and anger. He reminded me of nothing more than a cornered animal. Now I was in danger. His eyes flickered towards the gun cabinets. 'Give it to me,' he said in a low measured voice.

'No,' I said.

Colour rushed back into his face. 'Damn you, what do you want? How much?'

'I don't want your money. I want you to confess to Inspector Walker.'

'You're mad!'

'Perhaps, but if you have not made your confession to the police by mid-morning tomorrow I will hand over Miss Flowers's diary. Inspector Walker seems like an intelligent man to me and I am sure he will see fit to ask some

156

searching questions. At the very least your career will be ruined when it comes to light that you were duped by your secretary, who was committing treason under your very nose.'

Fairchild lunged for a gun cabinet. The doors rattled, but did not open.

I did my best to pretend I had known this all along. Perspiration dripped down my back. My heart hammered in my chest. I felt curiously light-headed. He turned and darted towards me, but I was quicker. I overturned an occasional table in front of him. He stumbled and fell. 'Do you think I would approach you alone like this if I had not taken precautions?' I said. 'As you guessed, I am not the only member of security here. My colleague has the diary. If anything happens to me it will still be handed to Inspector Walker and you will be charged with two counts of murder.'

'You bloody witch! Damn you!' He got to his feet, brushing down his trousers. 'You think you've got everything covered, don't you? Well, if I go down, I can tell you I'll take this project with me.'

'It's already been compromised,' I said, 'but it would be better for all concerned if you confessed to murdering Miss Flowers in a fit of jealousy.'

'Why would I do that?'

'Mr Leech,' I said calmly.

Fairchild clutched his head. 'I have to think. I have to think. There has to be a way out.'

I didn't know if he was talking to himself or me, but I said, 'You have until tomorrow. 11 a.m.'

He stumbled to the door like a sleepwalker and after dropping the key three times finally managed to let himself out. I waited a good ten minutes before I followed him. I knew that desperate men were liable to desperate actions.

Accordingly, I made my way to the kitchen as fast as I could and determined to keep in company with one or more of the servants until tomorrow morning.

I hoped that morning would bring sense and clarity to the situation. However Merry and I were awoken early by a banging on our door.

'Get up!' said Susan. 'We've been robbed.' I rushed to the door, but she was gone before I could get it open. Merry and I scrambled into our uniforms and headed to the kitchen. We found Rory pacing back and forwards in front of the range and Jock clutching his cleaver.

'Did either of you unbolt the front door?' he barked.

Merry and I both denied this categorically, but my heart sunk. Rory, as ever, was far too perceptive. 'You're looking guilty, Euphemia. What have you done?'

'I was asleep in my bed all night,' I said honestly.

Rory gave me a hard look. 'I know you're behind this,' he said.

Susan hurried into the kitchen, breathless and red-faced. I can't see anything missing in the main rooms,' she said. 'The gentlemen are all still abed. Should I wake them?'

'Not yet,' said Rory. 'We will now search the Lodge from top to bottom for signs of disturbance, so we can give a full report to our masters when they wake.'

'Should we do it in pairs,' said Merry, wide-eyed. 'I mean, they might still be 'ere.'

'If they are you lead me to them, lassie,' said Jock, waving his cleaver menacingly.

'I have no doubt they will be long gone,' said Rory, 'but you may search with Euphemia if you wish. Where do you think we should look, Euphemia?' he asked.

My mouth was dry, but I managed to say, 'The gun room.'

'But all the guns are locked away,' said Susan.

'You haven't been in there yet?' asked Rory. 'Then let us all go and look. Euphemia has a way of knowing about these things.' The latter was said more as an accusation than as a compliment.

We all trooped down there and, as I had feared, one of the cabinets had been shattered and a gun removed.

'What now, Euphemia?' asked Rory.

'We should check if any of the gentlemen is missing,' I said softly.

And of course, Mr Fairchild was gone. The men searched for him without even pausing to take breakfast. With awful irony they found him at eleven o'clock, floating in the loch, his head shattered by a blast from a shotgun.

Epilogue

Of course the police launched a full investigation, but it had hardly begun before it was shut down. The official verdict was death by persons unknown, but it was also unofficially allowed to be known that Fairchild had killed himself and that the verdict was to save his children and young wife further embarrassment. Miss Flowers's demise was recorded as death by misadventure. The Kiel Canal project vanished overnight.

Bertram told me that Rory claimed to have tracked down the mysterious forest-dwelling man during the search and reassured me that whatever he was, he wasn't German.

It was a sorry party that headed back to Stapleford Hall. We were barely through the door when Richenda rushed up to me.

'Oh, thank goodness you're back,' she cried. 'We have so much shopping to do! Hans is taking me on a world tour for my honeymoon and you're coming too. He's trying to get tickets for that new ship, the *Titanic*. It's going to be wonderful.' She embraced me.

Behind her I saw Rory delivering a letter to Richard Stapleford and the reaction it provoked. 'He really has resigned,' I said.

'Who?' asked Richenda.

'Rory.'

'Well, he's got the experience now. He can go

anywhere he wants. I think he's got the right idea. I can't wait to get away from this place. Come on. The automobile's waiting for us outside. We're off back to the Mullers' house.'

Bertram gave me a little wave as I was ushered out the door. He mouthed, 'See you soon.' I wasn't so sure. It felt like my little world was coming apart all over again.

**Other titles in the
Euphemia Martins Mysteries**

Coming Soon

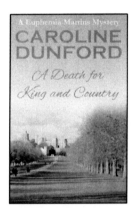

For more information about **Caroline Dunford**

and other **Accent Press** titles

please visit

www.accentpress.co.uk

For news on Accent Press authors and upcoming titles
please visit

http://accenthub.com/

Lightning Source UK Ltd.
Milton Keynes UK
UKOW02f1952071114

241279UK00001B/13/P